History of **ART**

History of *ART*

stories

~~MARGARET LUONGO~~

Margat Luongo

*For alice,
with all best
wishes,
Margat*

LOUISIANA STATE UNIVERSITY PRESS

BATON ROUGE

Published by Louisiana State University Press
Copyright © 2016 by Louisiana State University Press
All rights reserved
Manufactured in the United States of America
LSU Press Paperback Original
First printing

Designer: Laura Roubique Gleason
Typeface: Adobe Jenson Pro
Printer and binder: Lightning Source

Library of Congress Cataloging-in-Publication Data
Names: Luongo, Margaret, 1967– author.
Title: History of art : stories / Margaret Luongo.
Description: Baton Rouge : Louisiana State University Press,
    [2016]
Identifiers: LCCN 2015035402 | ISBN 978-0-8071-6302-3 (pbk. :
    alk. paper) | ISBN 978-0-8071-6303-0 (pdf) | ISBN 978-0-8071-
    6304-7 (epub) | ISBN 978-0-8071-6305-4 (mobi)
Classification: LCC PS3612.U66 A6 2016 | DDC 813/.6—dc23
LC record available at http://lccn.loc.gov/2015035402

The paper in this book meets the guidelines for permanence
and durability of the Committee on Production Guidelines for
Book Longevity of the Council on Library Resources. ∞

For Bernard, Tom, Pete, and Bernadette—
The first storytellers

Contents

The War Artist 1

Word Problem 17

The Confused Husband 33

Magnolia Grandiflora 37

Seeing Birds 58

Exile 63

In This Life 72

History of Art 86

Foreground 93

Fine Arts 107

The War Artist Makes God Visible . . . 111

Repatriation 115

Chinese Opera 122

Girls Come Calling 124

Three Portraits of Elaine Shapiro 128

Acknowledgments 177

Notes 179

History of **ART**

THE WAR ARTIST

"When do I start?" the war artist asked.

The captain glanced at his watch, his thin lips pressed into a sliver. Thirty seconds passed.

"Today," he said. From down the hallway a pistol shot rang out, followed by the sprightly pop of a champagne cork. "Right now, in fact." He handed the war artist a neatly folded uniform, saluted her, and walked out the door.

The war artist heard the jingle of the captain's keys and the solid thunk of the thrown bolt. She tried the handle, but it wouldn't budge. Looking through the small window, thick glass meshed with wire, she saw the gray of another metal door across the hall. She knelt and opened the slot, near the floor, and peered through it. "Hello?" she called. The hallway's fluorescent lights buzzed.

She turned back into the room. Tattered mobiles of jets and helicopters stirred busily in the artificial breeze of the air handlers. She sorted through her footlocker and bins of supplies. The office was stocked with her favorite materials, and for a moment this reassured her. Among the bins she found a fifth of Jack Daniel's and two shot glasses. Slices of light shone through the skylights. A small fluff of cloud passed over the sun. She changed into the fatigues the captain had left, sat at her drafting table, and waited.

She sketched to pass the time and to exercise her hand, soldiers in action poses that resembled her son's army men. The fatigues felt stiff. The room was so quiet that the scratching of her pen seemed to fill it. She drew her surroundings—a boring exercise, but an exercise nevertheless: a cot, a footlocker, a metal desk and chair, an easel, all done up in the sandy shades of this war's theater—dry sand, wet sand, oil and sand, dirt and sand. She wondered what her children were doing, and checked her watch. They'd be walking home from school with their father, chatting in their high-pitched voices. They'd stop for a snack along the way, something wholesome or not, depending on her husband's mood. They might yet expect to find her at home. She wondered when she would be deployed. She had told the children it was an honor to serve as the nation's war artist, that she owed it to the soldiers to do a good job. The weight of her new responsibility—to make the war comprehensible to those who couldn't witness it—exhausted her. She rested her head on the table and dozed.

During her nap, her civilian clothes disappeared and more fatigues arrived, along with an MRE and a pistol. She held the gun away from her, dangling it by the butt between her thumb and forefinger. She glanced around the room. Where to put it? Away, she felt, was the only safe answer. She assumed it was loaded. She would get the captain to take it away. In the meantime, for safekeeping, she placed it in her footlocker, nestled between mosquito netting and a poncho.

She turned her attention to the MRE. Three thousand calories, the package said. My, the war artist said. She had hoped for an itinerary or instructions for her deployment, but there was nothing else. She sketched the bulky MRE in its thick beige plastic, using watercolor pencils to finish it, and she tacked it on the wall over her cot. Better. The room had needed a little something.

She had only had a moment to admire her work when a thunderous booming shook the room. She covered her ears and cowered behind her easel. Another explosion followed, then the rapid fire of guns. The war artist curled into a ball and shielded her head with her arms. Sirens and shouting filled the hallway outside her door. More gunfire, more explosions, a moment of silence. She was panting. Then the screaming began, and cries in a language she didn't recognize, beseeching cries of a woman. It sounded as though someone had reached into the woman and pulled out her insides. The war artist understood from the sounds that the woman pounded on the chest of a soldier, all the while screaming about her children.

Focused intently as she was, she failed to recognize the sudden silence. It occurred to her that she might have been listening to a recording. The war was being fought elsewhere, not inside a government building. Yet a particulate substance floated in the air and coated her fatigues. New cracks crawled up the walls and around the skylights, and occasional chunks of plaster fell. The war artist beat her fists on the metal door and shouted, "Hello? Hello?" but no one came. Her arms and legs trembled. Dust from the newly cracked walls tickled her nose, and she sneezed into her sleeve.

No one came to explain what had happened. The war artist set to her pencils. She drew quickly, with harsh movements, fragments of the scene she had heard. The face of the mother filled an entire panel, her mouth a terrible wound. The soldier occupied his own panel, away from the mother, his arm raised in a half-realized gesture of comfort. Apart from these, she described a mostly empty space for the children: a faint horizon line with nothing above or below it save a few flecks to signify earth and a wisp of cloud for sky.

―――

She slept lightly, and in the night she woke to weather. The breeze at first was not unpleasant. She lifted her face to the hot wind, and it ruffled her hair. Particles of something fine swept across her face and forearms, clinging to each strand of hair. She shut her eyes against the graininess. The wind increased, ruffling her easel pad, scattering her kraft-paper sketches and gathering them up again in a whirling spout. The dust stung her skin and worked itself between her lips to coat her gums. She pulled herself into a tight ball and waited out the storm. Ink bottles pelted her, pens and pencils skittered across the floor, and charcoal sticks exploded against the walls, adding their powder to the air.

When the storm ended, everything in the room was coated with a layer of the finest sand she'd ever felt. Impossible to wash away, it burrowed under her watchband and worked beneath the wire of her brassiere. Everything she touched was coated in grit. When she sketched, she pressed her fingers into it on the shaft of the pen. Each sheet of paper became a kind of sandpaper. Eventually, the sand infiltrated all of her inks and paints so that everything she made contained it: the portraits of her husband and children that she drew from memory; the lakeside landscape of her family's summer home; a still life of her children's lunch bags and schoolbooks. When she blinked she felt it; too insignificant to induce tears, it stayed put. When she ate, it crunched like glass between her teeth. Each day, more sand blew in on a hot wind from a great furnace.

<hr />

Over the next few weeks, boxes of treats arrived from her family and friends who thought she was at war: pulverized cookies, melted Power Bars, outdated magazines, sunblock, salt tablets. She painted pictures of whole cookies and tall frosty milkshakes. She made pastels of ice cream sundaes, as cartoonlike in their sumptuousness as centerfolds. At night, and only after she felt she'd made a good-faith effort to produce, she reread letters from her family. Small details thrilled her: buying tomatoes at the farmer's market; making pancakes at home and setting off the smoke detector; the neighbor's cat darting in the open door and surprising everyone with a live mouse.

She, in turn, had little to say—and little she could say. Her first letter—"Dear Family, Your letters and pictures delight me! I still haven't been shipped overseas and am in fact very near you. . . ."—came back to her, with instructions to avoid mention of her location. The letter was returned the very day she'd passed it through the slot to the soldier who delivered her meals, packages, and letters. She became adept at concealing the truth without actually lying: "Dear Children, Very hot here, and the sand gets in everything! I must have eaten a bushel! It's strange to draw something as dry as the desert with watercolor pencils, but I find it my preferred medium. Be good to each other, and mind Daddy. All my love, Your Mommy."

The war artist tried to keep in shape by drawing and sketching, but she had grown tired of her room as a subject, and she could only draw so much from memory and desire. She found herself re-creating bland desert landscapes and predictable wartime tableaux, lifted from movies she'd seen. She requested newspapers and Internet access, via a note to the captain. The next day, several postcards skittered across the floor, having been flung through the slot. All depicted the desert around Las Vegas, circa 1950.

"What's this?" she called through the slot to the soldier. She could just see the butt of his rifle as he walked away from her down the hall. She was in the habit of calling after him. "Fresh fruit would be nice!" when another MRE thunked to the floor. "Thank you!" she'd call when he dropped off her packages and letters.

She flipped through the postcards, making sure she hadn't missed something more relevant. The last card had stuck to one of its mates, the edges of the canceled stamps interlocking. The front side showed a spangled showgirl dressed like Uncle Sam in fishnets and plunging neckline. On the reverse, written in faded

India ink, she read: "Very hot here! Sand everywhere. Eating bushels. More, love." The war artist swore.

"What am I supposed to do with this?" She heard a phlegmatic click from a corner of the room. She spun about, trying to locate the source. Then a different sound, a pattering, followed by a rushing swish of sand, spilling from the sprinkler heads above her. For the rest of the day and all through the night, the sand rained down. She found an umbrella in her footlocker and held it above her while the sand swirled and drifted in the manufactured breeze. Goggles protected her eyes. The heat in the room intensified until the war artist was forced to strip down to her briefs and brassiere.

By the time the storm ended, about a foot of sand had fallen. She cleared her tabletop and desk, shook out her linens. Her cot now was flush with the ground, and she kicked sand into her bedding any time she moved near it. The new landscape was awkward to walk in, and she found herself ill-disposed to do anything. Bourbon improved her frame of mind.

She was seated thus, in her underwear, sipping bourbon, when a young man in civilian clothing arrived. Sweat plopped from her chin and nose onto the blank paper in front of her.

"Hello," he said, offering his hand. "I am your translator."

The war artist wouldn't move from behind her table, so the translator staggered through the sand to her. His slick-soled shoes slid and pitched him forward into the war artist's table. They shook hands.

"There's nothing for you to translate," the war artist said. Patches of sweat blossomed on the translator's dress shirt. "I'm the only one here."

The translator held up his hand. "I get paid either way."

She offered him a drink, and he accepted. He sat cross-legged on the ground. She pulled on her trousers, and the translator explained the proud history of his region, the many accomplishments of his people, as well as the colonization, infighting, and religious oppression. The war artist rolled out fresh paper, and she drew a mural of the images and events the translator described. He kept pouring as he spoke, becoming more and more comfortable moving in the sand as they drained and he refilled their glasses. She looked at him from time to time; usually he stared off into a corner of the room, as if he could actually see the times and places of which he spoke. His slight accent felt lush to her, a spice she had never smelled or tasted. She felt she could slip inside the scenery she drew—the dusty streets, the ornate mosques and busy markets. She doodled away at some clouds and didn't notice that the translator had stopped speaking. When the lull of his voice subsided, she looked up to find him gazing at her. The expression he wore looked a little hard, but she couldn't read it. She looked back at the many feet of paper she had covered. She blushed.

"You've inspired me."

He rose and looked down at what she'd drawn.

"They knew about perspective before anyone else did, you know," she said.

"Who?"

The war artist smiled. "Your people," she said.

"That's all for today," he said.

She walked him to the door of her office, hoping to catch his scent, which she was sure would be exotic and thrilling: a spice or incense, some flower or plant unknown to her. All she smelled was sweat and booze. The soldier came and ushered the translator out.

The war artist painted after the translator had gone—ancient monuments he'd described and some she imagined, all to convey the past grandeur of the place. She fell asleep quickly, relishing the warmth emanating from the sand.

During the night, she woke to the sound of a helicopter hovering above her room. She threw back the covers and trudged to the skylights. The ground seemed to buckle under her feet. The pens on her drafting table jumped and fell nib-first into the sand.

The helicopter abruptly flew off, circled, and came back to hover somewhere very near. The war artist gazed up at the two sky-lights framing the night sky, rectangles of inky dark and nothing more. She lay down again, and each time the helicopter hovered, her sternum vibrated. Her ears tuned to the sound of the slicing blades, and she fell asleep, her organs humming.

⚏

The next day, she requested coffee for the translator's visit. He had mentioned a specific kind—cardamom. The coffee was delivered in a china pot with pink rosebuds. The cups matched. Not quite right, the war artist said, and she and the translator laughed. The war artist shook her head as if to cast her hair away from her eyes, but she meant to clear away last night's noise. Her body had re-corded the thumping whir, muffled and interior. She smiled at the translator, worried that her new sound might leak out.

"Today," the translator told the war artist, "I will tell you about my family." He clasped his hands behind his back and told of the economic hardship and the violence that had brought him to her country. In vague terms, he spoke of separation from his par-ents, his wife, and his children. The war artist felt heat rise on her cheeks. She had thought him too young to be married with chil-dren, and the fact of his coming to her room had given her a pro-prietary feeling.

The translator walked alongside the previous day's mural, which the war artist had tacked to the wall. He spoke of oppres-sion under the previous regime, the hardships and terror of the current war. Occasionally he fell silent and stared at his shoes sinking into the sand. Mostly, the war artist respected his emo-tions and waited for him to gather himself again. The translator stared at the palace the war artist had rendered, its gates open to a garden of orange-red flowers. Without speaking he lowered him-self to the ground and sat.

"So you help our government for the sake of justice?" the war artist said.

"Justice?" The translator looked down at his lap. For a moment, the war artist was afraid he couldn't continue, and she was sorry to have pried. He nodded. "I am very tired."

After the translator had gone, the war artist painted a new city, a new country—what might rise up like a field of wildflowers after this war: industry and parks; roads and public transportation; schools and universities; hospitals and laboratories, all peopled by rational, clear-eyed, hopeful citizens. What this new civilization could accomplish—and how the rest of the world would benefit from its example—once the dust had settled!

She made herself eat a light supper, a small portion of her MRE, and practiced sleep hygiene with renewed zeal. She had grown accustomed to the cot and the unfamiliar sheets, the sand and the lack of scent. In the dark, she heard the rattle of her murals on the walls, shifting slightly in the breeze from the fans: the good sound of work, of something made. She thought of the murals someday hanging in a museum or other public building, alongside ancient friezes from palaces destroyed by war. Drifting as she was, the hard rolling sound didn't trouble her. In fact, followed as it was by another hard something rolling, and another, the string of sounds was quite soothing. The hard, round things rolled in the hall, up against her door, and that reminded her of ocean waves lapping, until the explosions came. The sound tore through her ears, and blossomed red—fuller and fuller, pushing through her head, chest, and bones.

When the waves of sound receded, she lay on her back, rigid and panting. Every part of her felt shattered, her atoms and molecules reassembled imperfectly. The sheets were cold and damp. She thought of her youngest son, how he'd wept through his shame of bed-wetting. She rose to change the linens, staggering sideways, her inner vibrations throwing her off-balance.

On the third day, the little rosebud teacups rattled in their saucers as the war artist poured the coffee. Everything was bright and sharp—except the translator, who lumbered in with no stories to tell. The two sat across the room from each other, sipping. The translator's eyes were vague and unfocused. The war artist felt her gaze harden. At the very least, he could give her something to work with. They both had jobs to do, and despite the ringing in her ears and the ache of unease in her bones, she wanted to get on with it. She placed the cup and saucer on her desk and took up her usual position at the drafting table. She rolled fresh paper across it, picked up her charcoal, and cleared her throat.

"The heat's getting to me," the translator said.

The war artist raised her eyebrows. The man did look ill. "I thought you'd be accustomed to it."

The translator's head dipped on his wilted neck. His eyelids fluttered, showing the whites. The war artist jumped up, broke out a cold compress from her first-aid kit, and clamped it to the back of the translator's neck.

"They never get the humidity right," the translator said, loosening his tie. "Anyway, I'm from Boston."

The war artist sat down again at her drafting table. Over the translator's shoulder, the bright colors of her murals blurred. She sloshed herself a bourbon.

"You lied?" she said.

The translator removed the compress from the back of his neck and applied it to his forehead. "Those aren't lies," he said. "That's a lot of people's truth."

"Are you an actor?" the war artist asked.

"I'm a graduate student," the translator said. "Engineering."

The war artist sipped her bourbon, then threw it back. "What's your language?"

The translator shrugged and shook his head. He had an uncle, he said, who had lived in Dubai for a while, whom he'd gone to visit regularly, and he had his training, which helped to pay his way through school.

"This is a fucked-up situation," he said. "I tell stories of a life I haven't lived, and you make pictures of a war you haven't seen."

The war artist poured the translator another drink. "You can't leave," she said, "until you tell me something I can use."

She sat at her drawing table and prepared to sketch. "Now," she said. "Do you have a girlfriend?"

The nontranslating translator nodded. "She is Hindi and was born in Calcutta—"

"Stop." She pointed her charcoal at him. "I want the truth."

The young man looked away, smiling faintly. "Her father was a physician in Iran during the Shah's reign. They fled to South Florida—"

The war artist stood. "Imagine I point a gun at your head." She demonstrated with her thumb and forefinger.

He stared at her. His black-brown eyes looked wide and innocent. The war artist retrieved the pistol from her footlocker and pointed it at the translator's head.

"Do. You have. A girlfriend?"

"You don't have to do that," he said. "I'll answer your questions."

She shook the pistol at him.

"OK," the young man said. "She grew up in Worcester. She's terrible at math. She makes good potato salad. We fuck in her parents' bed while they're on vacation. We did it once on her stoop and the neighbor across the street saw, and my girlfriend still cries about it."

The war artist straddled her chair. The facts steadied her. "What else?"

"We're supposed to get married when I graduate."

"Supposed to?"

"She wants to."

"But you don't."

The young man looked at the ceiling. "It's not that I don't want to, it's that I don't think we'll be ready. She's never dated anyone else, and how can I be sure—how can she be sure—"

The war artist raised her pistol and tried to fire into the ceiling. Nothing happened.

"Squeeze again," he said. "Like you mean it."

She fired into the ceiling several times, which caused her to flinch and cry out. The translator shielded his head. He waited for the rain of plaster to stop before answering. "I don't want to marry her," he said. "She's boring, except when we're fucking."

The war artist stared up at the now-crazed skylights. "I should shoot you," she said.

The nontranslating translator shook his head. "I know," he said. "I know."

In the end, she sent the young man away. With him, she sent a note to the captain: "I want to do my job. Let me do my job."

The next day a yellow form in triplicate, having to do with the discharging of her pistol, fluttered from the slot in the door to the sand. She used needle and thread to embroider her explanation: "It's a war."

≡

After she sent her translator away, the war artist so missed even incidental contact with others that the rosebud china service pained her to tears. She couldn't bring herself to smash the cups and pot. She made weepy studies of the trio until her sorrow bored the hell out of her. Better to make it big and lurid, this loneliness. She started on large paper, and painted quickly in watercolor couples straining to make themselves one, but the paper was too small. The edges antagonized her. She moved to the walls, covering over her murals with big powerful strokes depicting the most intricate orgy she could imagine. The figures blurred together, though the most disturbing image repeated itself plainly enough: men and women opening their jaws wide and stretching their mouths over each other's faces. She stepped away from the wall and felt the hunger and tenderness of the gesture: to want so strongly!

Every morning, she lined up her buckets and laid on more paint, until the figures were impossible to discern. When the wall glistened thick with color, she threw herself into it, smashed her cheek in the cool earthiness, and rubbed herself along the oozing surface. She rolled along the wall and moaned, pounding her fists until she felt a shattering ache the length of her body. At that moment, she thought she heard the static click of an intercom. She remembered the sound from grade school. She paused for the message. "Eh-hem," a voice said. Blushing, she pulled herself away from her painting. The war artist, slick with ooze, vowed to make herself and her feelings smaller.

⚊

She didn't see why she should eat since the food always tasted the same and it was so hot, and anyway everything had sand in it. So she ate only what she absolutely had to, and she watched as her stomach, upper arms, and thighs melted away. For the sake of something to do in between bombs, sandstorms, art making, and masturbating, she did push-ups and sit-ups. She admired her newly chiseled arms and abs. Fuckin'-A, she said to herself in the mirror. I am one bad-ass bitch.

She was an art-making machine: totally focused, she'd learned to manage the boredom, fear, loneliness, and lust. She had been bribing the soldier who brought her food; she made pastel portraits of his children from snapshots and school photos he provided. He sighed over them, opened the flap in the door, and shoved in a stack of newspapers. The newspapers were in Arabic. It was true she hadn't specified the language, but she thought her guard—for that is how she thought of him—was playing games with her.

She spent the day tearing the newspapers into strips. She set up her camera, took off her clothes, and carefully wrapped herself from head to toe in the strips of newspaper. She stuffed wadded newspaper in her mouth. Only her eyes showed. She left one arm free enough to work the camera's remote. She made a series of photographs and attempted to send them to her family, via the bribed guard. The next day, a new guard appeared, one whose hairless knuckles and hammy-looking fingernails promised no shenanigans.

She stayed in bed all day. She nibbled crackers, curled on her side, and slept. In the night, she woke and tore fresh white sheets of paper into strips, laid them on the floor, and took pictures. Then she went back to bed. She couldn't say what any of it meant, but she kept doing it, for ten nights by her count, until she realized she'd gone daft. She stripped nude, tensed her muscles, and stared down the camera. She made side and back views of herself, and printed these. She admired her muscles, tracing her finger along the new gutters of her body. With great care and precision, she tore her photos into strips and ate them. Then, using a very small screwdriver, she disassembled her camera. She spread the parts on a thick piece of pearl-gray paper and instinctively reached for her camera to document it. Oh, said the war artist, my. With a hammer, she smashed the parts of her camera, taking care to herd the wayward pieces. With a mortar and pestle, she ground the pieces into a fine and sparkling pile of dust. She tried letting the particles dissolve on her tongue, but they clung, coating her mouth and caking at the edges of her lips. The thing to do was wash it down, so she opened her bottles of India ink, and once she started it was difficult to stop.

Eventually they came. The soldier with the ham-like fingernails stepped matter-of-factly over her spatters of vomit. He helped her to her feet and led her gently down the hall to a room where the captain and other soldiers waited. The captain motioned for her to sit at a long table, around which the other soldiers sat. No one spoke. The war artist sipped water from the glass in front of her, rinsed her mouth, and spat on the floor. She was determined not to speak first. The soldiers stayed very still. The air handlers whirred. She glanced down at her briefs and became aware of her stink. In the two-way mirror at the far end of the room she saw herself: gristle, bone, and muscle dressed in a sweat-stained undershirt, wearing a goatee of inky vomit. She crossed her arms in front of her. She thought of her family and all the time wasted. Finally she spoke. "Am I to be debriefed?"

The oldest man in the room—the general—who sat across from her at the long table, smiled mildly. "What is it you'd like to know?"

He reminded her of her grade-school principal, willing to give only what information was necessary to answer the inquiry in the most meager way.

"Why did you keep me here?" the war artist asked.

The general removed his glasses. His eyebrows were gray and bushy. "We thought—we hoped," he smiled, "that you could show us something about the war."

The war artist felt a roiling burn at the base of her throat. "What did you learn?"

The general suppressed a smile. "You responded in interesting ways. We were touched by your . . . humanity. We admired your passion." He folded his hands in front of him. "Time for one more question."

Grit clicked between the war artist's teeth as she spoke. "Why did you keep me in that room?"

"I see," the general said. "We didn't want to hurt you."

Some soldiers at the table had gone red around their ears and necks. A fine crust of sand lined the uppermost ridge of a young man's ear. One young woman had an angry red stump for a thumb. The ham-fingernailed soldier, upon closer inspection, wore prosthetic hands. The war artist couldn't help staring. She wondered if his new finger fit the trigger. She imagined him working it into place, not being able to feel the resistance or gauge how much pressure was necessary to squeeze off one round or two. She watched the soldier so intently that she didn't notice the urge to sneeze coming on, and she neglected to cover her mouth and nose. She sprayed the soldier's new hands with dark gritty mucus.

"I'm sorry," she said. She started to wipe her nose on her forearm, but the soldiers on either side of her offered hankies.

"It's OK," the soldier said. He cradled his M-16 as he wiped his prosthetic hands. "It happens to all of us. It never goes away."

WORD PROBLEM

I.

Ten students attend the conservatory at a nationally acclaimed school of music.

Students **A** and **B**, male and female respectively, are naturally gifted singers for whom music is an uncomplicated joy. Whether or not they themselves become nationally acclaimed products of the nationally acclaimed school, they imagine that they will sing all their lives. Both feel sheepish about the nerve it takes to send oneself to a nationally acclaimed institution in order to devote oneself to a discipline that all but promises some version of failure. Even people who are very good probably aren't good enough. Frankly, they are a little embarrassed by their self-indulgence, but they have to get a degree, and it might as well be in something they love, something that doesn't yet feel like work.

Three of the students—**C**, **D**, and **E**—are insecure perfectionists who are fiercely competitive. Student **C** has an eating disorder and wears only black T-shirts and jeans. The other students suspect that he waxes his entire body because he has no arm hair. Student **D** is insecure about her breasts and wears extra-extra-large sweatshirts, even when conducting, which sometimes gets in her way. No one would care anything about her breasts, but she has made such a show of her horror of them that by the end of her third year she is known as "Tits." She has a beautiful voice, which she disavows, though she will sing Happy Birthday as long as a top and a bottom are available. Student **E** seems nice enough, and she actually is nice, though most of her peers suspect she is not as nice as she seems. Her parents have inculcated in her a faith that promotes tolerance and loving-kindness, so she mostly competes with herself. She has not played team sports, but she did march in band (tuba), so she knows what it's like to work hard with others. She took some grief as a girl playing tuba. She is very tall.

Red-haired Student **F** has a vibrant personality that she uses to mask the pain of growing up with overly critical alcoholic parents. People who don't know her well—and most don't—think she is intense but harmless. She goes to some trouble to remain harmless, as when she attended classes for one week posing as a man dressed as a woman. Some assumed devotion to *Rocky Horror*, others to whimsy or musical theater. Her friends, both of them, knew that her brother had punched the windows out of his bedroom and had just begun a long convalescence in a private hospital.

Student **G** possesses modest gifts but is even-tempered and hardworking. She knows she is good enough for certain things— teaching, for instance—but she also thinks she might be able to make it as a performer. She sees plenty of people waste their talent—it doesn't move them, they are lazy, or they refuse to take an interest to spite their parents. She also knows that some people are weird or assholes, or so crazy they can't get out of their own way. Some are full of self-loathing, and they sabotage themselves. She figures if she can hang in there, she will probably be successful. If pressed, she would admit that her dreams with regard to music making involve steady work and steady pay.

Student **H** is a well-adjusted genius. His parents love him and have been supportive of his musical activity from a young age. If asked, he would name having to quit sports as his sole lingering resentment from childhood. He was twelve when he injured his hand playing baseball and couldn't practice piano. You cannot serve two masters, his father said. But **H**'s body loved sport: the thrill of physical contact with other players; moving at speeds uncalled for in the rest of his life; poised, alert and waiting for the next play to unfold. Nothing in his life has equaled that feeling. When he plays music with others he experiences similar moments of anticipation; something is about to happen, and he can't predict exactly what it will be. He especially feels this when he sits in with jazz musicians, which he does as often as possible. It's like a pickup game, he tells his parents, though they don't know anything about basketball, except that it's a way for musicians to ruin their hands and embouchure.

Students **I** and **J** are smart—very smart—and they are assholes. After two semesters, each thinks he is the smartest person in the school. They no longer believe in music as it is typically defined. They are sure most people do not even hear what is being played. They are not allies; in fact, they take no notice each other. They tend to skip class, and the music they want to make can't be conjured in the practice rooms. **I** skulks around the trestle near the defunct paper mill, recording the sounds of trains coming and going in the blue hours. **J** writes evocative nonsense verse, which he turns in for every assignment, regardless of its relevance. His teachers assume he is having a breakdown or that he is stoned. Something is wrong with him, and it's not their fault or problem. He arrived this way, bright and unready to learn.

Students **I** and **J** know all about John Cage. They don't know that they are furious with him. They feel—and they are right—that they can never employ his logic in order to surpass him. They will always be re-creating his experiments on his terms. They can't articulate this, but John Cage is their father, and they would like to murder him. Each suspects, on an unconscious level, that he is not smart enough to metaphorically or intellectually slay John Cage. The alternative is to get good at something people might actually like. Thus their rage and despair.

II. Problems

Solve the following problems, showing your work. An answer key follows.

1. Twenty years after they earn their degrees, how many students make a living at making music?

2. How many graduates of the nationally acclaimed school of music become nationally acclaimed themselves?

3. How many students maintain an uncomplicated relationship to music?

4. How many students write jingles for television?

5. Which students suffer breakdowns and why?

6. Which students give up on music, and how long will it take them (in months) to conclude that they should quit?

7. Which students become parents who will NOT push their children into music?

8. How many students will answer questions about their musical training with rueful good humor?

9. Which students go on to become teachers who are thoroughly bored by their students?

10. How many students become music directors for their parish?

11. Do any of the students drop out? Which ones? Why?

12. Which student develops an intense nonsexual relationship with an older mentor, moving into her Manhattan apartment and spending a lifetime composing on her piano and traveling to Greece with her every summer of their life together?

13. Which student realizes, in his late forties, that he is gay and weeps for his effaced sexuality?

14. Which students, if any, go into politics?

15. Which, if any, become Republicans?

16. Which, if any, undergo gender reassignment?

17. In their spare time, two students are part of a string quartet that plays only works by John Cage. One takes particular pleasure in the vocal parts. The other wonders why anyone comes to their performances. He feels that he and the audience are frauds and somehow the fact that they perpetrate this sham together makes life more bearable. Identify the students.

18. Which students can't locate the source of their misery?

19. Which students become university employees?

III. Answer Key

1. Six students make a living at making music, twenty years after earning their degree: **G** and **H** as full-time orchestra members; **I** as a college professor; **E** as an assistant band director; **A** as a church music director; and **C** as a composer of popular music and lyrics. The nationally acclaimed institution takes few risks on the students to whom it grants admission.

2. Four of the ten become nationally acclaimed: **I**, the very smart asshole, for his organized sound projects in new media; **C**, the insecure and fiercely competitive perfectionist, for his popular music and lyrics; **H**, the well-adjusted genius, who has become principal violinist for a major city's orchestra; and **B**, the naturally gifted singer for whom music is an uncomplicated joy, for her power in local politics, which has galvanized grassroots movements across the country.

3. None of the students has an uncomplicated relationship to music, with the possible exception of the vibrant and red-

headed **F**. She most enjoys dressing up as David Bowie (Ziggy Stardust era) and fronting a Bowie cover band. This pleasure allows her to negotiate the unresolved feelings she has about other parts of her life. In other words, her musical activity allows her to keep living, which, owing to momentum and a certain kind of inertia, isn't as complicated as it sounds.

4. **C** has written jingles for television commercials. He enjoyed the nonsense rules imposed by the marketing people about demographics and "vibe." The work had nothing to do with him—it was simply a puzzle to solve as brilliantly as possible. One summer day during his one-year tenure as a ball-of-fire jingle writer, he woke up in a foam of white sheets, Big Sur blue blazing through the skylight, and he was finished with commercial writing, or this type, anyway.

5. Students **A** and **F** suffer breakdowns. Everybody saw **F**'s breakdown coming and thought it heroic the way she put it off so long. During this brief "rest," as she called it on the telephone with her mother—"I'm resting a few bars, Mother. I'll jump in when it comes round again"—she wraps herself in thrift-store sweaters and experiments with macaroni-and-cheese recipes, trading one cheese for another, trying different herbs, noodles, and toppings: breadcrumbs, store-bought and homemade; cornflakes; panko; tempura kelp. **F** nurtures herself with music, too: Carole King, Mahler, Varése, Bowie. Mostly, she stares off into space. Her two friends check on her. What brings her out of her funk? Not the art therapy, not the individual or group counseling, but a playwright friend of her brother's. He leaves a shy message on her answering machine: Would she read a part in his new play, the part of a waif-muse with supreme empathic skills? Intrigued by the idea of being supremely anything, **F** gets off the couch. She knows something about feeling what others

feel, having practiced a perversion of empathy with the alcoholics in her life.

The naturally gifted **A** loses it quietly, by himself. Anyone with eyes could have seen it coming. He has the best kind of breakdown: job quit, he drives to San Francisco, meets some nice young men, remembers who he is, and drives back East after a year's exploration of the flesh and grins of beautiful youngsters who vibrate with music and drugs. As the sun helps the body make and store vitamin D, so does this experience help **A** to make and store some unidentified substance that sustains him for a while.

6. Student **D** gives up on music entirely, toward the end of her junior year—about twenty-eight months after accepting admission to the nationally acclaimed school of music. She does enough to graduate. She marries, has children, and becomes an excellent conductor of household affairs. The children understand to do things her way, that it gives their mother great pleasure to see everything just so. Her husband knows his prescribed area of performance. He dreads the time—coming soon—when the children will prefer to pursue their own pleasures, rather than their mother's. Already the youngest intentionally loses the scarves **D** wraps her in before school. After the children, before middle age really sets in, **D** will have some work done to fix the one area of her life that still does not meet her standards.

7. **H** is the only graduate who will push his children into music. They are naturally gifted, he reasons, and he can teach them from an early age. By the time they reach adolescence, he'll know whether they have the passion and discipline necessary to sustain a lifetime of intense focus. He will allow them to play sports, and in that way—via a foul tip, an elbow to the face, or some other mishap—the decision might be made for

them. He imagines himself coaching, but he doesn't think he can stand occupying the sidelines. Instead, he considers the old-man league, exhausting his body until it aches, appearing in the kitchen, muddy, muscles wrung to quivering. But of course he can do no such thing; he supports his family through his job with the major city's symphony orchestra, and he cannot risk injury. Most mornings he rises early and runs alone—through the woods near his house, on the trails slick and fragrant with rust-colored pine needles, or in the neighborhood, rustling through fallen leaves. He imagines himself diving to make a play, plowing through a defender, swinging a bat, feeling the force of contact in his bones.

8. Only **C** and **D** will make jokes about their musical training, and they will make exactly the same kind of jokes, along the lines of "Well, they tried their best to teach me, but—" After his enormous success, **C** stops making these remarks. To continue would be disingenuous. **D** will remain a lifelong yukster on the subject of her aborted musical aspirations, it being her fault and no one else's. Every year, she writes a check to the nationally acclaimed music school's scholarship fund. In lieu of her alumna update, she pens a smiley face on the memo line of the check.

9. At different points in their lives, eight of the ten students find themselves teachers bored by their students or by teaching. Some work through the feeling and keep teaching; others run from the task, the way healthy animals flee the carcass of a fallen member of its species.

10. One student—**A**—becomes Music Director for his parish. He prides himself on providing excellent music for Mass, weddings, and funerals. No other parish has such a good liturgical program; in fact, **A** has been wooed by monsignors and bishops, all eager to procure his talents for their diocese.

At home, he tells his partner, "The Bishop tried to pick me up again. Apparently, I am irresistible." His partner glances up from the *New York Review of Books.* "You're being cruised by Christ. Don't you think that's a little weird?" **A** thinks about it, sits on the arm of the sofa where his lover reads, and says, "I take it where I can get it."

11. None of the students drop out, but **J** flunks out after his first year. **I**, who had just started to notice **J**, feels humbled for a moment, then angry all over again, though he can't say why. He only knows that he works harder; he doesn't ask himself any questions other than, "Am I working hard enough?" He attends every class, reads professional journals, practices in the practice rooms, haunts the music library when he finds himself with extra time, and keeps up with everything new while his professors teach him centuries of music history. Many years after graduation, he considers trying to find **J**, then thinks better of it.

12. **C**, though wildly successful, is still an insecure perfectionist. He does not know what he has done to deserve the unconditional devotion of his mentor. He recalls something his mother said while exhaling smoke from her long brown cigarette, somewhere in the neighborhood of her fourth and fifth cocktails: "The rocks in his head fit the holes in hers." This in response to another situation in another time, but he thinks it apt now, and he doesn't find it harsh or unkind. Rocks, holes—all that matters is the fit—and the outcome: good music, professional respect, material wealth, contentedness. His success and his enjoyment of it stem, in part, from his ability to create puzzles challenging enough for him to enjoy solving. His mentor delights in these games, and she waits to be amazed by what **C** produces, which spurs him on.

   C still takes a dim view of eating, so she prepares meals so suited to his palate that he can't resist them, and these in very small portions that simultaneously satisfy and create appetite. **C** knows his mentor has bested him in this arena. How clever of her to create something so desirable, in such limited quantities. He thinks once, watching her in the kitchen—slim, blonde, in her vintage pedal-pushers—that someone should have sex with her. Later, at dinner, he clears his throat between sips of chardonnay and suggests as much. A tiny forkful of risotto enters her mouth; she chews, swallows, sips from her wine glass. "It's not that I'm short-circuited," she says, and he notices how tiny she is, how little of her there actually is. "This," she says, waving her fork in a tiny circle at herself, "is a conservation project." The sun blazes in, hot on **C**'s cheek, and he has never felt so warm and content.

13. For many years, **A** feigned indifference to sex so that he could avoid sleeping with men. Through the kindness and patience of an extremely attractive man, who also happens to possess a lovely tenor, **A** has finally found himself in a steady intimate relationship. "We'll make up for lost time," his partner tells him when **A** bemoans all the youthful sex he missed. "You probably wouldn't have liked it anyway," his friend tells him, stroking his forearm.

14. **B** realizes that though she is gifted, she is unwilling to work as hard as she would need to in order to become exceptional, if that is even possible, and she suspects it is not. She is willing to work hard enough to teach at the primary or secondary level, but a brief stint as a junior counselor at a music camp leads her to the conclusion that this, to her, would be torture. Meanwhile, back home, her neighbors lose their jobs, their homes. At her parents' kitchen table, she hears about the teenagers' wages her neighbors earn at factory jobs in the new economy—people raising families, making less than she did scooping ice cream during summer vacations. Loading up on history and political science, she finishes her degree and

canvasses for local politicians, working into the early-morning hours at campaign headquarters, knocking on doors all weekend, rallying support. In the night, she wakes to find her fingers moving across the phantom neck of her guitar. Years later, while working late at the statehouse or drafting policy on a commuter flight, she'll regard the slimness of her fingers and remember their pressure on the strings; the smell of sandalwood comes back to her. She pushes herself harder, hallucinating from fatigue on boring stretches of road between campaign stops; bars of music and teleprompter text float amid the telephone wires and billboards. She hums what she thinks she sees before her and digs in her purse for something to keep her awake.

15. **D** marries a Republican and votes Republican, though she maintains her registration as a Democrat. Her husband does not know she votes Republican; he assumes she is a bleeding-heart liberal, and that is one of the things he loves about her.

16. None of the students undergoes gender reassignment, though **F** considers herself a cross-dresser. She lives in a college town on the side of a mountain in Tennessee, where people are gracious and appreciative of her gifts. They don't mind her turbulent bouts of inflamed fashion. They know to be extra kind, gentle, and appreciative as her hair color changes, heels rise and fall, sequins come and go. The extra kindness manifests itself in no outward change in their behavior toward her.

17. **G**, the modestly gifted student who is even-tempered and hardworking, neither lazy nor spiteful, weird nor crazy, plays cello in a quartet specializing in the works of John Cage. **H**, the well-adjusted genius, plays violin. Both are also members of a major city's orchestra. **H** is, as principal violinist, the boss of **G**. **G** approves; so does **H**. **G** feels perfectly secure, which is

why **H** is attracted to her. She is not intimidated by his talent, so he pursues her. **H** enjoys the look of impish delight on **G**'s face during their performances of the experimental work. **H** has no idea what the other musicians will do, and that keeps him coming back. It's fun for him, but he can't see how it could be much fun for the audience. Sometimes he ventures a sideways glance at the patrons and he sees looks of delight and surprise—and blank expressions, too.

18. **J** is utterly blind to the source of his misery. As a result he lashes out, not even having the sense or good grace to channel his anger into wry self-deprecation, which would make him much easier to take. He fails to grasp the utility of sublimation. Every year, he petitions the nationally acclaimed school of music to award him a degree, based on his "real-world" experience, most of which has nothing to do with music.

    D, on the other hand, knows the precise nature of her problem: It's her cowardice. She does not want anyone to see her trying and failing—and she is sure she would fail. Even if she could get past her fear of shame, if she cannot have things as she pictures them, she does not want them.

19. **E**, **F**, and **I** become university employees.

    E becomes assistant director of the marching band at a mid-sized midwestern university. She loves her work, loves how hard the kids work. They arrive during summer break, weeks before the other students, and they practice hours every day during the school year, fitting in homework during the times when the other kids play video games, get drunk, or fix their hair and makeup before going out to get drunk. Sometimes, when **E** is poised on the grandstand at practice, her arms raised, a vision appears before her: a mound of used reeds, discarded mouthpieces, dented mutes, bent stem-cleaners— decades of band garbage, spit-slick and breath-moistened, that she herself has plucked from the practice field year after year, touched with her bare hands. Other times the phantom odor of well-worn band uniforms fills her nose—B.O. so deeply hormonal that the stink clings to the inside of **E**'s van weeks after she's delivered the uniforms to the dry cleaner, giving **E** the experience of piloting a crotch or an armpit down the road, day after day. But on the grandstand, **E** does not hesitate. She cannot keep the students waiting in the blazing sun with their heavy instruments. Later, she does not wonder about the meaning of these phantasms.

F becomes a counselor at a university in the South where students still refer to northerners as "Yankees"—with irony, of course. The students could not be more polite and well-mannered. In her spare time, she plays music with some of the faculty and students. Because the students graduate in an orderly manner, they are always coming and going from **F**'s life. She becomes attached to them, which she knows is sad. Her best friend is a gay playwright-in-residence who weeps for the lack of gay men on the mountainside where they work. They host rip-roaring costume parties, to which students and their parents are invited. **F** thinks how phony is the divide between teacher and student, adult and—what? Quasi-adult? The students are simply people with less experience and knowledge, though in many cases that is arguable. She knows that some of them know things she doesn't, and though they are younger, they have skills and experience beyond her. She tries to get to know them as individuals with their own peculiar interests and desires. After many years, she has yet to meet a truly boring student. They seem vanilla on the outside, with their brand-correct clothing and sunglasses and their fit physiques, but she knows that on the inside she will find what makes each of them unique. These excavation projects excite her, and she hoards the strange details of their lives, for no particular use but her own wonderment. In fact, she finds that the duller the student's exterior, the more faceted and sparkling the interior. Sometimes the blander ones are buried so far inside themselves their very appearance in her office exhausts her. They have no idea what's inside them. They move through their days like scared animals responding to stimuli.

She takes them on adventures. Unusual activities in unfamiliar settings disarm them; they talk, and they reveal themselves to themselves—and to her—without realizing it. Rock climbing for the timid; nursing orphaned wildlife for jocks; whitewater rafting for the repressed; thrift-store shopping for the fastidious; headstone rubbing for the overly ambitious. She remembers one student in particular, always impeccably groomed: peach picking with this one, over summer break; the student refused to meet her parents on the island of their habitual summering, so F and the young woman plucked just-ripe peaches and made pies with intricate cutouts and latticework. While rolling dough in F's elegantly unremodeled and un-air-conditioned kitchen, the young woman recalled sitting by her baby sister's crib each night, watching the child breathe. She'd fall asleep on the floor, night after night, until her parents sent her to boarding school. Now her sister attends school in Paris. The two meet in Europe for holidays, spurning their parents; their parents pay for the trips, including a suite in a five-star hotel, though the sisters sleep in the same bed. F glanced from time to time at the girl's face as she told her story, noting the color creeping into her cheeks, her hair going lank around her face from the heat and steaming pots of peaches. "What should we do with all this *pie?*" F asked. "Give it away," the girl said, "to whoever wants some."

I is a full professor of music and new media at a major research university. He is hot shit. For a while, he perceives no ironic distance between who he is and who others take him to be: hot shit, inside and out. He remembers the particular kind of asshole he was in school and realizes that in some ways his confidence and focus benefitted him, and in others did him harm: He performed poorly in subjects he didn't care for, and no one reached out to guide him because he was such a jerk. He spots students like him—actually, they flock to him. As gently as possible, he tries to convince them to be less like him, but the evidence is more persuasive than his words; he invites them to his home to make music and they see all his instruments, the electronic equipment, the artwork. He disappears in the middle of the semester to travel to international conferences to which he has been invited as distinguished guest. He watches them watch him, those assholes, and he doesn't know what to do. "I've been lucky," he tells them. "You're a fucking genius," they say. Because of him, they believe in themselves utterly, believe they will one day prevail.

I remembers **H**, the real fucking genius, who could take music centuries old and make it new. When **H** conducted, they were capable of surprising themselves and each other. He thinks often of his fellow students. No one had more heart than **F**; every event touched her, and she transformed it and her emotions into wondrous performances. He wonders how she's getting along, what gifts she bestows on whom. And **J**, that crazy bastard. Did he harness his epic rage? He thinks about **D**'s toughness, how they tormented her about her big shirts. No one could sing like her. **G** and **E** worked like devils, never showing the signs of wear or resentment that often come from working harder than everyone else. **A** had been so humble and sane; he was probably running an orchestra somewhere. **B** was changing the country, motivating people to get off their asses and really make a difference. She could have done anything; she could have been the college professor. But she was helping others in what, to **I**, was the nobler cause. And **C** made millions with his ingenious tunes—popular music so fresh and surprising that **I** had to pull his car to the shoulder to listen once or twice. C pleased himself and yet managed to delight others. I could not say the same of his own work, which mostly no one outside his small circle cared about. This is what he'd wanted.

Even so, I knows that he has had more success than he deserves. To compensate, he devotes himself to nurturing his students; maybe they will be better than he is, in every sense; maybe they will become people who fully deserve their success. In this way, over the years, I becomes less and less like the asshole he once was.

THE CONFUSED HUSBAND

He met the woman he was to marry, but she didn't have a limp.
The old witch who'd read his cards had said his wife would have
a limp. He had understood the crone's message: His bride, lovely
and perfect in every other way, would have a malformed leg; his
life would be one of hardship, working to support and care for her.
He told the crone, It doesn't matter. I'll love her anyway. He felt
very noble. The witch swore at him in her dialect and spat in the
dirt. Obviously, she had not been so lucky.

So he was surprised when he met his bride-to-be, that she
didn't have a limp. In fact, he found her exquisite in every way:
smooth olive skin, black wavy hair that shone, and deep brown
eyes. He admired her back, the way her muscles moved under
the bodice of her dress as she drew water from the well. That she
didn't have a limp troubled him, but only for a while. When they
walked in the square, he noted the approving glances of his neighbors. At their wedding, amid all the dancing and well-wishing, he
sensed the pleasure people took from the match. For a shadow of
a moment, a chill shivered his spine, but then it was time to carry
his new wife home. The husband ran through the streets with his
bride in his arms. The wife was wrapped head to toe in a veil made
by the women of the town, and the scent from her glowing skin
steamed up through the delicate lace. The husband couldn't wait to
get her home. "I love you! I love you!" he cried. "I love *you!*" replied

the wife. The husband threw the wife down on their bed and unwrapped her. They embraced, and they weren't careful about it, because they were young, and their bodies were perfectly sound.

Years passed, and the husband did not grow into the man he had envisioned. Instead of a quietly suffering, tolerant, and impoverished man who was generous with his crippled wife, he became a prosperous and influential leader in the town. The wife came from a good family, and their good fortune rubbed off on him. He didn't have to think very hard; every choice he made was correct and delivered to him more wealth, security, and respect. When the townspeople had problems or a difficult decision to make, they went to him, and he was thoughtful and decisive. The wife, as she aged, grew even more beautiful. Her back never bent under the weight of her chores, and the husband still found her irresistible. He often sneaked home in the middle of the day to interrupt her housework with his advances. She always returned his interest. Sometimes the husband would pretend to change his mind, so the wife would pretend that she insisted, and she'd chase him through the fields until he let himself be caught. Their many children always survived infancy, and they grew to be strong, clever, and cheerful.

After a time, the husband grew weary of his role in the town. No matter how much advice he gave, no matter how many problems he solved, always people came to his door with their sorrows—often the same people over and over. Their suffering was like a disease from which they could never recover. He hated the way they humbled themselves, their eyes downcast. Defeat whined in their voices, and the sound burrowed under his skin. Sometimes, when he saw them approach, he slipped out the back door. As he fled, the husband would recall the life he'd previously thought his destiny, and how willingly he would have embraced it, had it been his fate. Why didn't these people understand their role—to bear up with quiet dignity, to persevere nobly?

He stalked home after one such episode, having wandered the

surrounding hills of the town in an attempt to calm his mind. His wife had left a lantern burning at the gate, and the smell of rabbit stew drifted out to him. He watched her move—setting the table, pouring the wine. He remembered the life he had imagined: trudging home from the fields to care for his invalid wife, supping on a broth of root vegetables, never quite having enough, always a little hungry. He'd fall asleep quickly, sleep hard, and wake up with stiff muscles. He'd cook breakfast for his wife, massage her aching, deformed limb, and go off to the fields for another day of labor, satisfied he'd done right.

But here were his beautiful, healthy, strong wife and their beautiful, healthy children. What did that make him? Lucky. Where was the nobility in that? All his material goods, his wife and children, *he* knew, if no one else did, that he'd done nothing to deserve them. How ill-suited he was to his life, how it chafed. He understood suffering and knew how it was done, far better than he understood happiness and good fortune. Hadn't he been raised by his poor mother for a life of hardship? What now was this? He had grown soft. He'd had no chance to show how tough he could be—not like his beseeching townspeople, who had every opportunity to prove themselves. He felt cheated.

During supper, when the children giggled happily and sang snippets of their songs, he roared at them. They were surprised, but not afraid. His wife thought he'd had a difficult day or wasn't feeling well, so she sent the children to bed early. She gave the husband some brandy, and he threw his cup on the hearth. "Can't you see?" he cried. "You're killing me!"

He became critical of the way she did things around the house. He was more inclined to stay home than tend to business, so he had more opportunity to find fault. At first the wife thought he might be sick, and she called the doctor. The husband swore at the doctor, and chased him away with an axe. The wife couldn't see anything wrong. She ticked off in her head all the problems they didn't have: no deaths in the family; they didn't owe money;

the children were healthy and smart enough. "I don't understand you," she said, with great sympathy. "Please don't worry. Everything is fine. You're a good husband, a good father."

The husband shook his head and wept. Had he married a simpleton? Lately he'd been a terrible husband and father—drunk, irritable, impatient.

"I don't know why you're doing this to yourself," the wife said. "You have no right to feel sorry for yourself. You *have everything*. You've been *given everything*."

With that, the husband roared out of his chair and ran at his wife. Not one to take a beating, for she knew she didn't deserve it, she ran away from him. He chased her through the fields, shouting, "You're killing me! All of you! Killing me!" The wife shouted back, "You're insane!" It was while she shouted over her shoulder at her husband that she stumbled into a gopher hole and broke her ankle. The bone never set properly, and ever after the wife walked with a limp. She didn't let it get her down, and she carried on— gay and industrious as ever.

The husband took his wife's misfortune hard. He stayed indoors and neglected his business. His children avoided him, and the townspeople no longer trusted his judgment. Eventually his business failed, so the wife packed their belongings, took the husband and their children, and moved in with her parents. The wife's parents felt lucky to have a house so filled with life. They treated the husband humanely, with love and kindness, as they would any invalid.

MAGNOLIA GRANDIFLORA

I would like to tell my sister Janice about the dream I had last night. I was in the kitchen, getting ready for Christmas dinner or some other holiday meal. I opened the freezer to find the skulls of our parents staring back at me. I panicked. The peas were freezer-burned. I had forgotten to replace the scotch, and where was my father's favorite ashtray, the resting place for all his cigar-ends? I squinted at my parents' eye pits. Behind me, Dean muttered something about keeping the door open too long. I blinked, and before me sat a bag of hoary peas, a few disks of pork, and an ice cream cake from the Fourth of July that had half-melted and re-formed as confectionary slag in the bottom of the box.

I would like to tell Janice about this when she comes over to-night with her husband, Paul, but I probably won't. We're having New Year's Day at our place this year. Dean makes ham rolls at the kitchen table while I set up the bar. I wipe each thick shot glass and plunk it down on the sideboard. The glasses came from Dad's bar, and they are heavy and solid.

"You should put out the teapot Janice gave you," Dean says.

For Christmas, Janice gave us a ceramic teapot. It looks like something a Who from Whoville might excrete. It's very original. It just doesn't go with anything. I say as much to Dean.

"It would be a nice gesture, though, to put it out."

I consent to this and put it on the counter. "On a scale of one to ten, hideous."

"Be nice," Dean says.

"I'm always nice."

He turns to show me his raised eyebrow.

"What?" I'm already imagining packing the teapot and its tray into a box and dropping it off at Goodwill.

Janice and Paul come exactly on time, bearing topiary. The topiary is surprisingly normal and lovely: an elegant tower of holly balls in a gold-painted pot. "I love it." I'm so taken with it that, for a moment, I block the door and Paul and Janice can't get in.

"I really, really love it." I take the topiary from Paul and turn it to inspect the glossy dark leaves and red berries. Dean gently tugs on my sleeve. I hop away from the door, letting Paul and Janice enter.

"Well," my sister says, managing to sound both smug and incredulous, "I'm glad you like it."

She has brought black-eyed peas—a southern tradition, she says. Paul is from Louisiana, and he wants to make us Pimm's Cups, a New Orleans specialty. "I don't want to interfere with your traditions. If there's something else, I . . ."

"No, no!" Dean and I won't let him finish. I hate that Paul is so careful with us, that Janice has instructed him to be so, and that he is kind enough—or scared enough of Janice—to do it.

"Pimm's Cups all around," I say.

Paul worries about his parents while we listen in the living room. His parents ran a grocery in the Marigny, downriver of the French Quarter, until they retired a few years ago. They moved to Mobile and hate it, so they're moving back to their old neighborhood in the spring. As we chat, I squint at the floor. The glare of the waxed hardwood gives me a headache. Dean is an ardent polisher and waxer, whereas I prefer things scuffed.

"I mean, they're old," Paul says. "What will they do there?"

"Travel?" I say, because I imagine that's what retired people do.

"They only like New Orleans," Janice says. "It's ruined them for other places."

"So they'll be happy there," my sweet Dean says. I kiss his forehead from where I sit on his lap.

"You're breaking my legs," he whispers.

I hop up. "I think I need another of these New Orleans specials."

Paul gets up to make our drinks.

"I wish they lived closer," he says. "I worry about the call in the middle of the night—not getting there in time."

"Well," I say, "they have to go sometime."

Janice snorts. "Nice."

Paul nods. "You're right."

"Anyway," I say, "it's not like they're ever really gone."

Dean looks tired, and Janice says something quietly to him that I can't hear. Paul seems pensive. I change the subject.

"Where did you get the topiary? It's charming."

"Paul made it," Janice says.

"Really?" I touch Paul's arm. "I had no idea you did such things."

"Neither did I," laughs Paul. "I just woke up one morning with this image in my head. Luckily it was a Saturday. I went right to the nursery for materials."

"If it had been a workday, he never would have done it," Janice says.

"That's right," he says. "I would have been at my desk at 7:00 a.m."

Paul is one of those brokers who works very, very hard, not the kind that comes to work at noon in golf clothes.

"He did great business over the holidays," Janice says. "The angels were really popular. We were at the festival three hours, and we sold out of everything—bells, angels, mistletoe balls, reindeer."

"I wish I had known," I say. "I would have gone."

Janice blushes, and Paul gives her a look that tells me he thought I did know.

"It slipped my mind," Janice says, looking at her lap. "The holidays! So crazy."

Paul and I ignore her. "If things keep up this year," he says, "after Christmas I can probably quit my job."

"Wow." I look at him, shaking my head. "I mean really—wow." Can you imagine? Waking up one morning with an idea like that—something simple like topiary—that changes your entire life? For a moment I imagine the contents of my parents' shop, now my shop, and its cartoon disappearance: poof! Then nothing. I insist on opening a bottle of champagne to celebrate Paul's new talent.

Janice follows me into the kitchen. She leans against the counter. "I see you've got the teapot out."

"Yes!" My enthusiasm suggests I will profess my love and admiration for it. "It's very original."

"I didn't think you'd like it," she says. "But the topiary. You do surprise me sometimes."

"I think Paul's talent is marvelous."

"It is nice," Janice says. She's more subdued than usual, and when I look up from the cork I've been trying to pop, she looks lost, as if there's a vast sea before her and she doesn't know where to fix her rudder. The look scares me, so I ask about work. Janice runs a small vocational agency; she helps career castaways and misfits find their true professions. Sometimes they just find jobs; sometimes they find they are totally different people than they'd imagined. Once, a fifty-five-year-old woman, laid off by the battery factory where she had worked for thirty years, took a test and discovered she would make a fine game warden. In two years she was a park ranger in the Keys, carrying a rifle and protecting herons, gators, and park visitors. In another success story, the marketing director of a software company found satisfaction as a mail carrier. Janice helped him realize that his unhappiness stemmed from too many hours indoors.

I offer Janice champagne in the old-fashioned saucer-type glass. "Who have you helped lately? Tell me a good one."

Janice sips, shakes her hair back, and says, "I don't help anyone."

"Pish-posh," I say, and she flinches. "You're fabulous and you know it."

She takes up the hem of my organza hostess apron—one that belonged to our mother—and fingers the lovely diaphanous fabric. She traces an embroidered daisy with her thumb, and before I can stop her, she's poked straight through it. I slap her hand away, clocking her with the enormous diamond dinner ring on my right hand. She looks at me, shocked.

"Sorry," I say. "I didn't mean to hurt you." A red splotch blossoms on the back of her hand.

Janice licks her lips, a bad habit that chaps her skin. Our mother used to yell at her for it, that and gum chewing. "Dry rot," she says, looking satisfied. "Guess you'll have to throw it out."

"I have no intention of throwing it away. I'll fix it," I say. "No harm done."

We stay up until three, buoyed by Pimm's and champagne. In the living room, Dean and I sit opposite Janice and Paul, and I look from Paul's topiary to Paul, and back again. I've never seen a new thing with such importance. The clusters of leaves—glossy and compact—seem ready to burst from their arrangement. The brushstrokes in the gold paint reflect tiny worlds of lamplight; each stroke shows Paul's hand. Yet it is a very simple thing. I look up to find Janice staring, too.

The next day, I have a headache. Dean straightens his tie while I lie across the bed in my running clothes. Soon I'll head to the track, where I'll work on the coach of a local triathlon club. His mother died recently, and I want to make myself available to handle the sale of the estate. It's delicate business. One can't appear eager.

After I drop Dean at the private high school where he teaches history, I drive to the track in my father's old Mercedes. It's butterscotch-colored and doesn't require as much maintenance as you'd think. I have fond memories of riding in the backseat when I was small, on our way to the homes of the recently deceased, where my father or mother would manage the sale of generations' worth of heirlooms. Much of my business comes from connections my parents made long ago.

Coach is himself on the downhill slide of life, though he's as healthy as a man approaching seventy can be. Sometimes he jogs with me during my slow warmup. He makes fun of the young girls who turn out in their perfect outfits—the white singlets and powder-blue running shorts, their hair pulled into tight ponies. "See that girl?" He points to a young woman stretching at the perimeter of the track. A few young men—actual athletes with rocklike quads and sinewy calves—stand around her, smiling. Once practice starts they'll forget about her.

"I see her." I already know the punch line.

"I've never seen her run."

"You should ask her to join the team." I mean this to be funny.

"I should," he says. "I will." He veers away from me, running at his true speed, far faster than a man his age should be able to. He has such an intentional gait—he means to get somewhere, the way he pushes off from the track, putting it behind him. He pulls up beside the girl, introduces himself. The young men break away and hit the track. Coach will have the girl on his team in a day or so, and she may last a few weeks or even a few months. She's young, and probably not used to pushing herself or staying with things after they've stopped being fun. She may run too hard, start off too quickly, injure herself, quit. But he'll get her for a little while, and who knows what he'll be able to do with her. I've seen him take regular people—insurance agents and human resource officers—and turn them into competitive athletes. He jogs with the girl around the track, talking and laughing with her. The sun glints off the windshields of the cars in the parking lot, and I feel my jaw tighten; I'll have another headache later.

After I've run six miles through the neighboring streets, after Coach has done what he can stand to do with the girl, we reconvene at the track for a leisurely stretch. This is where our best talks occur. I tell him to let me know if he needs assistance with his mother's estate. He doesn't answer for a while. Then he says, "What did you do with your parents' estate?" He knows my parents are dead, though they died at different times: Dad first, heart attack, then Mother, lung cancer. "I mean, that would be weird, selling your parents' stuff."

We're both on our backs, not looking at each other.

"I still have it. Dean and I live in their house."

"What—you just fit your stuff in around theirs?"

I imagine the disaster that would have been. "We got rid of most of our furniture. It was cheap."

"What about your husband's stuff? Didn't he have parents who gave him things?"

Dean had rooms full of blond modern museum-type chairs and tables that didn't go with anything.

"Dean has his own room. We converted the carport. He keeps the things he can't part with there."

"So you have a whole house full of things you can't part with, but all his stuff has to fit in the carport?"

"It's not a carport anymore—it's really a very nice room. Why are you making this a problem?"

He doesn't answer my question. "My girls are coming this weekend to take what they want. I'll let you know if I need your help after that."

We make plans to meet for a beer after his practice on Thursday, while Dean's taking a course for recertification.

At home, in the foyer, the glare from a mahogany picture frame slices into my field of vision and I wince. The oval frame holds a photograph from my grandparents' wedding, New Year's Day,

1906. Neither of them smiles, in the European tradition of leaden portraiture. Would it have been impossible for them to smile—on a happy occasion? Would it have killed them?

In the shower I try to rinse away my headache. I'll make some calls at the shop, keep some appointments. Collectors come for the vases, paintings, and jewelry the dead have left and the living don't want. I have auctioned entire households of furniture—secretaries stuffed with crinkled letters in foreign languages, pantries full of home-canned tomatoes, beans, cabbage, and soup, moldy sporting equipment—white leather skates, wooden tennis racquets, scuffed bocce sets and rusted horseshoes. And over everything the thick dust, the heavy, living smell of thriving mold and mildew. In my office, stacked in bookcases with glass doors, sit tins and leather albums of unlabeled family photographs and daguerreotypes. Researchers from the university come to paw through them, searching for items of cultural interest, anything that will justify their hypotheses. A pale graduate student came by once to see my collection of "families engaged in leisure pursuits." I gestured to the cabinets, told him I hadn't sorted the photographs. He offered to catalogue them by period and subject, but I told him no, the families should stay together. He shook his head, repeatedly, all week as he came every day to sift through the photos.

At my desk, I unfold the newspaper and glance at the front page. Someone's young son drowned in a swimming pool; a teenager drove her parents' car into a tree. I think of the girl's room, her plastic beads, ribbons from cheerleading or equestrian, those collages girls make when they are bored, lonely, or angst-filled, the inevitable diary. The boy's room: posters of sports stars—hockey, baseball, basketball—and the gold and silver trophies. Maybe a musical instrument, bought on installment, with a dried-up reed. I turn quickly to the obituaries and make note of likely candidates. I keep a stock of tasteful sympathy cards, though truthfully there's no such thing. I include my business card, which describes my services in plain terms. I mail about thirty of these a week and attract the interest and business of about one in thirty. Often I get calls six months, a year, or even three years after the fact. It takes a while for the family to pick through what's left. Sometimes they never do; the boxes sit for years until someone decides it's time to move, or a new baby arrives, and the boxes of diapers and toys crowd out the dead.

I'm making out the cards when the bells on the front door chime. A fairly young man enters. He wears a cheap-looking suit—the jacket hangs crooked and the pants pull across the front. The shirt is pale yellow and looks like part of a Catholic boy's school uniform. In his hand, he holds one of my cards. He clears his throat when he sees me behind my desk.

"Are you—?" He waves the card at me.

I put down my pen. "I am."

After a little hitching motion, he clumps toward my desk. His pants are short and show his dark-brown socks when he walks. I imagine he sprang up late for work and threw on clothes without a single glance at the mirror. He tells me his parents are dead and he wants an appraisal of their possessions. They lived in a house just outside town, in a swank subdivision, built on a rise in the woods—the kind of place where executives lived side by side with successful artists and everyone had cocktail parties. My parents would have attended parties there, but I'd never had a client from this neighborhood.

I agree to drive over with him. He lays his hand on the dash of the Mercedes and leaves a sweaty palm print.

"Nice car."

I see him calculate its worth. "Thanks. What did your parents do?"

The man sneers. "My mother was an artist, and my father was a collector."

This seems promising. "He collected art?"

"He thought it was."

"Are you an artist?"

He laughs out the window, then turns to face me. "Do I look like one?"

I want to say, You look like the manager of a fast-food joint. He is, in fact, the manager of the Popeye's on Main Street, where he presides over fryers filled with catfish nuggets, big pots of gumbo, and baking sheets of dry, buttery biscuits. I remember his pale unwholesome face floating under the grease hood with all the brown faces of the cooks.

His parents' house is filled with junk. The house itself is lovely—all windows and natural wood. On the main level, we pause by a wall of sliding glass doors to take in the view of dense green growth. Live oaks strung with blue-gray Spanish moss make lacework of the sky. Saw palmettos scratch and rustle. The top-heavy pines stand stiff, upright—the straight men of the hummock. I imagine he must have fond memories of such a lovely place.

"Will you be moving in?"

"I'm selling it," he says. "You want to buy? I'll sell it to you right now."

He probably can't afford the taxes, but his voice tells me he wants to be rid of it for other reasons.

"It is a fine house. Maybe you should show me the other things first. I'd have to talk to my husband." I don't want to insult the place by outright refusal.

"Don't wait too long if you're really interested. These places don't go on the market often. I mean, somebody has to die."

He turns, and I follow down a cool, dim hall. We pause in an open doorway. Huddled in the room like terrified rodents, obsolete computers and monitors stare at us. The father collected vintage Macs and PCs, and now their gray cases and blank glassy screens sit waiting for their caretaker to come and—do what, exactly, with them?

"He was going to make the Mac Classics into fishbowls and sell them on e-Bay. This was just a hobby," the son tells me.

A little farther down the hall, he opens another door. The hulking, matronly forms of antique clothes washers greet us. "Ditto for these," he says.

We climb creaking narrow stairs to the upper level, and the son leads me to the father's workshop. The doorbell rings, followed by loud pounding. "That's the egg man," he says, and he turns abruptly to answer the door. The two talk, but I can't hear what they're saying. The son returns, out of breath from the stairs, looking a little embarrassed. "Can I borrow two dollars? I don't have enough cash, and I need to pay him."

"Sure, no problem." I reach into my purse.

He snatches the bills and says "Thanks."

I realize he's not sheepish at all; he's in a hurry. He probably has to get back to work. I guess he told the egg man about his father's death right there on the doorstep. I turn back to the room. On the desk is an egg. Someone has been painting it but has left off work. The bottom half is still white; the top half displays an intricate floral pattern rendered in glossy jewel tones. To the left of the desk sits a long wooden table, its surface covered with eggs that have been drained of their insides and covered in pigments, some with geometric patterns or flowering vines, others with animals. A rooster with majestic russet plumage catches my eye.

The son returns, slightly red-faced and out of breath. He hands me two cartons of eggs. "These are yours. I forgot to have delivery stopped."

I stare at him.

"My father paints them? Painted them."

I agree to take the eggs but nothing else. I ask him to tell me about them, and he rolls his eyes.

"It's a Ukrainian thing. All the oldsters go for it. The house was always filled with this old-country crap. You should see my mother's paintings."

I tell him I'd like to see his mother's paintings.

"She made her own paint," the son says. "She was a loon—they both were. She used the yolks my father blew out of the shells."

The mother had painted a series of a cuckoo clock—fifteen smallish canvases. Though each clock has all the numbers it needs to mark the passage of time, none has hands. Instead, each face reflects a different quality of light. Some have a cool feel, as if only weak daylight washes the scene. In others, the canvas glows gold—lamps keeping dark away. In the murkiest, twilight nearly obscures the Roman numerals—a faint edge shows here and there—and the clock itself seems to lurk on the darkened wall, marking time in a private way. Among these hang the more subtle deviations, small slices of the day captured for examination. I wonder what the boy did while his mother worked all these many hours, if he played patiently nearby or if the mother worked quickly, so as not to be late picking him up from school.

"Do you have more of your mother's art?"

"This is it. The rest she sold."

"Why not these?"

He puts his hands on his hips. We both regard the paintings. "She said it reminded her of me—my childhood."

I drag my gaze from the paintings to the man. "What did she mean by that?"

He exhales through his nose. "I have no idea."

"Well," I say, "they're lovely," though what I mean is they're full of sorrow. "I'll take them."

"Great," he says. "Good."

I hadn't noticed at first, but the pink background of the paintings matches almost exactly the pink of the wall on which they hang. The wainscoting also matches.

"What happened to the clock?"

The man is already removing the paintings from the wall. "I broke it."

He agrees to pack the eggs and drop them off at the shop. I

take his mother's art with me. I already know where it will hang: in the foyer where my grandparents' wedding photo hangs over the mahogany table, beside the grandfather clock. The paintings need a wall to themselves; all of those items will have to be relocated.

Inside, I hear an abrupt sound from Dean's room, the sound of someone rising quickly from a chair. Dean shuffles into the foyer and stands there, still in his school clothes, home three hours too soon.

"Are you all right?"

On his face, a look of recognition appears.

"I am sick," he replies. His arms hang at his sides. I've never seen him more inert, like a machine waiting to be turned on.

"What happened?" I go to him and touch his wrist.

"Nothing happened." He glances past me at the paintings. "What are those?"

I explain and he nods. He moves to sit on the couch. "Aren't you tired of it?"

I panic a little. "I don't know what you mean."

He loosens his tie. "I can't breathe."

"I'll open a window." As I move past him, he takes my hand. "I quit my job."

Suddenly, I am no longer married to a history teacher. I sputter for a moment about the outrage of his not talking to me first, but before I can even begin to form the sentence, I drop into the chair opposite him and say, "Oh." Practical considerations aside, "Oh." So many questions bubble up and dissipate. I wait for Dean. He tells me he's been seeing Janice—professionally—behind my back, instead of taking recertification classes. He isn't made for teaching history. He's meant for working in nature.

"That's how it always works for her clients," I tell him. "They'd all be happy if only they could work outdoors. Don't you think that's a strange coincidence?"

He doesn't respond.

"Are you going to be a game warden or a mail carrier?"

Dean shrinks into himself. "I'm going to be a naturalist." When I don't respond he continues. "I'll give tours of the parks and tell people about the land—its trees and plants and birds. It's a whole other world."

It occurs to me that Dean will still be a historian, but now he'll be historian of the trees, hills, hummocks, and creeks. I stand and straighten my skirt. "If this is what will make you happy, good for you." It comes out more forcefully than I'd anticipated, and Dean seems even more depressed. "This will make you happy, right?"

"I just wish," he says, then stops.

"What?" I say. "You wish what?" I feel a snarl rising in my throat and I want to snap, "You dare to wish *what*, exactly?" He doesn't say anything. I turn away and busy myself clearing the wall for the paintings. As I reach for my grandparents' wedding portrait, I feel my lips pucker into the sour pout I suspect may be responsible for the lines I've been seeing around my mouth lately. I try to catch my reflection in the portrait's glass, but it's too dark to see anything so faint. Dean helps me move the grandfather clock and mahogany table to our bedroom. We hang the paintings together, and I think about their creator. I try to read these artifacts from her life. I feel something like hope, but I don't know why. We stand back to admire the effect.

"I like them," Dean says, and he takes my arm. "I really like them. You have a good eye."

I wave away the compliment. "Pish-posh," I say. I'm pleased that he feels something for the paintings. I watch him from the corner of my eye, my husband, this unfamiliar creature. Janice's fraudulent counseling feels predatory now—not the stuff of amusing stories—as if she had practiced on all those hapless wanderers until she could get to us. I had no idea Dean was lost. Why didn't I? And why didn't he come to me first?

Over the next few weeks, Dean is transformed into a bigger presence in the house. Correction: he has a presence in the house. He goes for long walks and returns with pinecones and dried needles, leaves from deciduous trees and live oaks, all of which he deposits around the house in my mother's Waterford and Limoges. I don't raise an eyebrow. When he's not looking, I touch the pinecones and leaves. He's keeping a small journal—he draws pictures of the trees and plants he sees on his walks, writes the common and Latin names beside each. The book is quite lovely, its pages swollen from humidity.

I never knew he could draw, didn't realize he has been drawing all the time we've been together. I remember the maps he made for his classes, to mark out the old boundaries and show lines of battle, but it never occurred to me that he drew these. Now I remember they contain too much of Dean to have been traced. He included icons to help his students remember something about each country: the Netherlands marked with a windmill and a bicycle; France identified by the Bastille and a mob cap; Italy, the Colosseum and an olive tree. I am sorry for his students that he won't be teaching anymore. I remember how excited he was to discover that they could learn, that he could teach them.

He schools himself now, by making this book. Along the edges of each page he has drawn pictures of the insects that pollinate the flowers, the birds that nest in the boughs of the trees, the animals found nearby. He draws full miniatures of each tree, flower, plant, and shrub, along with close-ups of their leaves, stems, petals, and nuts. For the magnolia ("Southern Magnolia, *Magnolia grandiflora*"), he has drawn the tree in our front yard, with a partial sketch of our brick-and-cinderblock house in the background. In the margin, he has drawn a small Dean in tie and khakis, and me in a flippy skirt and running shoes. I laugh at the sight—I would never wear running shoes with a skirt. He has made me angular and girlish, about ten years younger-looking than I am. My freckles are there, and I'm smiling. I tap my finger on my colored-pencil self. She looks to be having a fine time.

I start to notice things, too: the longleaf pine needles collecting at the base of the Mercedes's windshield; the mashed pinecones everywhere in the street; the fine grains of black and white sand embedded in the asphalt of the driveway; the dried magnolia flowers that look like the hulls of giant seeds. On the way to see Coach Tuesday night, I listen to the Mercedes's engine, a loud diesel purr I usually drown out with the radio. I hope Coach tells me he doesn't need me for the job, that he's handling it himself. I shouldn't have brought it up. He's already sitting at an outdoor table when I arrive.

"Where's your new recruit?" I say as I sit down.

He shifts in his seat a bit stiffly and angles his face away from mine.

"Boyfriend troubles," he says.

Coach has a cut high on his cheekbone, and there's blood in the white of his eye. I don't ask about it. Instead, I tell him about the paintings. He agrees that they sound interesting and tells me I should contact one of the local galleries to show them. He doesn't mention his own business, and he seems chagrined about something. He allows himself to be distracted by the ring on my right hand, the dinner ring my father gave my mother for their eighteenth wedding anniversary, the one that left a red mark and scratches on Janice when I backhanded her. It had come from an estate sale and is something meant for after five. The center diamond is emerald cut—a whimsical and misguided choice. The emerald cut doesn't have enough facets, so the brilliance of the diamond is never brought forth. It is an extravagant waste. The stones surrounding the center stone form a ring so wide it grazes my knuckle. After my mother died, I put it on as a joke and never took it off.

"Is that real?"

I assure him it is, and I tell him the story of the ring.

"Why the eighteenth anniversary?"

"He didn't see why twenty was more special than eighteen or fifty better than forty-nine." I shrug.

"No offense," Coach says, "but that thing's tacky."

"That's kind of the point," I say, though I'd forgotten that. "I don't even like it."

Coach laughs. "Why wear it?"

"It's funny?"

We sit silently for a moment, Coach with his white hair blown away from his face by the breeze of his perpetual forward motion, and me squeezing my fist until the ring digs into the sides of my fingers.

"I got rid of my mother's stuff this weekend."

I breathe deeply and sigh.

"Packed it all in boxes and hauled it over to Goodwill."

"Good," I say. "Really." I feel relieved for both of us.

I walk him to his car. In the darkness of the lot, in this transitional place where neither of us will look each other in the eye, I can't refrain from asking. "Soooo," I say.

"Sew buttons," he says.

"What happened to your face?"

"Ah—that." We get to his car and he hauls himself onto the trunk. He leans back against the rear windshield. I settle next to him. The car is still warm from the day's sun.

"Shelley—"

"The nonrunner at the track?"

"Yeah." He's about to tell the story, but he interrupts himself. "I don't understand young women."

"Yes, you do. Tell the story."

"She wants to get a piercing."

"OK."

"In a place with a lot of nerve endings."

I am pained for Coach. "Is that how she put it?"

"I won't repeat what she said. It's too dumb."

I imagine her giggly and coy, hinting around, then blurting something vulgar or childish. "Why did she tell you?"

"You know how people talk when they run."

I inventory all the things I've told Coach while running, and I vow to be more circumspect. "Did she say why she wanted it?"

"She said she wants to feel more."

I wince. "So what did you say?"

"I said, 'Ouch.' Then I told her I could help her feel more."

"Oh, no."

"Then she kissed me."

"Did you stop her?"

"Not right away."

The car feels very warm now. We sit a while in silence.

"Anyway, I told her I meant that I'd get her running hard every day. Then she'd feel—her feet, her shins, her knees, her hip flexors, her quadriceps—not to mention the sense of accomplishment. She thought I was making fun of her."

"So she decked you?"

"She ran off crying. Her boyfriend—"

"If she has a boyfriend, what's she doing at the track all the time?"

"Sometimes one boyfriend is not enough. It takes a village, you know."

"Well," I say, "I'm sorry that happened. You don't deserve it."

"Thanks."

"You should have stopped kissing her sooner." I give him a playful backhand above his knee, and he grabs my hand. He holds on and rubs the back of it with his thumb. I wait to see what happens. He places his thumb over the ring and presses down. "Get rid of this thing," he says. "You're too old for costumes."

Swallowing is hard. "Get rid of it?"

"Stop wearing it."

I relax a little. I expect him to assign me a penance of miles and intervals, but instead he invites me to breakfast Saturday after a long run. I frown at him. "You're up to something."

He gets up, stiff-legged. "You're paranoid." He stretches. "Get rid of that thing, seriously. It's ugly."

I know he's right. I've associated myself with something in poor taste, that isn't even funny anymore—or never was. On the way home I consider throwing it out the window, but that seems excessive, an extravagant gesture, much like the ring itself. And what has it ever done to me? At the thought of selling it, a steel door in my brain slams shut. The ring will not be sold. In its ugliness, it is unique. Stopped at a light, I slide it from my finger, open the ashtray and drop it in. My fingers feel much slimmer. I can make a tight fist, and each finger can feel itself against its mates. "For the right occasion," I tell the ring, and then I correct myself. No more lying: the right occasion doesn't exist. What did my father think he was making fun of?

═╪═

Janice comes by on Saturday after my run and breakfast with Coach. She walks quickly from her car to the door, her long black hair whipping around her. We've been talking about throwing a fancy party for Valentine's Day, at which we would unveil Paul's new topiary: Cupids with bows and arrows, and ivy trained to climb on hearts and X's and O's. Since Dean's revelation, however, I have been avoiding her calls. She lets herself in, and I stop her between the kitchen and the foyer.

"Dean tells me you think I'm a phony," she says.

"I said that all your clients end up with outdoorsy jobs. It's an observation."

She walks past me and stops at the place where her teapot was on New Year's Day. "I see the teapot's gone."

"Janice," I begin, but she won't let me finish.

"Never mind. It doesn't matter."

Then she makes apparent the reason for her visit. "Why don't you come to my office? We can help you."

I'm still holding the plate I was about to put away when she walked in, and I grip it a little tighter. I would like to change out of my running clothes, shower, and nap. Dean is out for a long walk in the woods with his sketchbook. We've been grilling out in the evenings, and he shows me his book. It's filling with his gently colored drawings of our little world. Every day I look forward to seeing what Dean sees, our same surroundings, but different. Everything has changed. I cannot tell Janice she is a fraud.

"Did you see the new paintings?" I walk to the foyer and she follows. "You were in such a state when you came in." Standing before them, I feel an affection that spills over onto Janice, just because she's near.

"Where did you get these?" she asks, as if I have done something very bad by having them. I tell her. She shakes her head and gestures to the canvases. "You can't tell what time it is."

"It's the light, Janice." I am touched by her literal-mindedness. "You have to look. Each one is different."

She stares at the paintings. I wait and wait for her to understand.

"I have no idea what you're talking about. I never know what you're talking about."

It occurs to me that Janice might never ever understand. I wonder how I will feel about her if this proves true. "Janice," I say, "the teapot was ugly. Dean thought so too."

She gives me a tired look. "What does Dean know? I tell him it's his destiny to be a naturalist. I think he'll go back to school, get some useful degree, but what does he do? He makes drawings of leaves!" She spits out this last as if it's a piece of poisonous bark.

It occurs to me that Janice might like to work in nature. I tell her.

Her face goes pink. She seems to quiver just beneath her skin, as if she is made of something molten, about to burst and shower us with her liquid fire.

"You know what? You pain me. This place"—she gestures to the foyer, the walls, the house—"you're rotting in here. Can't you do something new with your life?"

I look past Janice and catch my reflection in Mother's silver tea service. My cheekbones appear in the shoulders of the coffee urn, high and white, and my mouth stretches long. My eyes are dark pits. I imagine pounding each piece flat with a rubber mallet—the coffee urn, the teapot, the sugar bowl and creamer—and hanging it in pieces on the wall, where I could gaze into the shallow, fragmented pools of myself. I feel the plate in my hand—part of Mother's Wedgwood set. The blue band around the edge is heavy with decoration, layers of raised enamel under my fingertips. The pattern crowds the edge of the plate. In the center, a variation of the pattern repeats itself in tight circles. I see quiet dinners Janice and I have taken with our parents, the dishes and glasses, crystal and china, salt cellars and candlesticks of the dead all around us. The smell of the shop presses in: the faint smell of mildew and mold, in my own home—in my parents' home—so familiar, so comfortable. I look Janice in the eye, raise the plate over my head, and hurl it at the floor between us. She flinches and twists away. Splinters of blue and red china flare around us, already something new.

SEEING BIRDS

Equipment

The only essential equipment for seeing birds is a pair of eyes.[1]

Where to Look

In the woods behind your home, among the reeds around the drainage pond, in the trees that line the streets in your neighborhood; downtown on the sidewalks, by the side of the road when you're driving to work, overhead as you walk through the lot from your car to the office, out the window when you stare over your coffee cup on break. On vacation, wherever you are—at the beach, the lake, the cabin in the mountains.

How to Look

With your eyes, not your memory. Your memory can't be trusted. You think you've seen birds, and maybe you have, but can you describe the last bird you saw? A silhouette of a buzzard (or was it a hawk?) as you drove through the countryside to your in-laws' house; a starling, somewhere—aren't they everywhere?—one of those tiny pied creatures pecking at the asphalt in front of the bagel shop early Sunday morning. These generic birds that you've seen thousands of times, you don't really see them anymore, and when you think of them, your half-powered brain plugs in a vague image—enough to satisfy the urge to recall *bird*.

Why Look?

If you aren't looking, what are you seeing? Your coffee? The window glass? Air? The white field with black letters on your device's screen? In terms of visual diet, a starvation ration.

Parts of a Bird

Resist naming the parts of the bird; words dispel the image. What does *wing* look like? Or *bill* or *tail*? No one image belongs to *wing* or *bill* or *tail*, so naming is useless for seeing.

Bird Classification

Birds can be classified one of two ways:
1. The bird before you now.
2. All other birds—figments of your poor memory and imagination.

NOTE: Even the bird before you may be compromised.

How to Look

Forget everything you think you know about birds. Forget the word *bird*.

Family Tree of Birds

In North America alone, one can find nearly fifteen hundred species of birds.[2] If I say to you *plover* what image comes to mind? How about *pied-bill grebe* or *merganser*? My guess is nothing comes to mind. You could attempt to memorize the exact features of these birds—fifteen hundred species in North America!—but you're not going to. You might make an attempt by keeping a book on your nightstand and paging through, looking—really looking—at a few color drawings or photographs before bedtime, memorizing the shape of the bill, the curve of the throat, breast, and belly, the parts of the wing and its various shapes, the feet—webbed, feathered, grasping, perching—the silhouette of the head. That seems unlikely, doesn't it? You'll only ever see about one hundred species in your own territory,[3] and you probably won't even remember to look for them, unless you set aside specific time for that.

Taking a Scientific Approach

Are you a scientist? I think you are probably not up to the task, but I admire you for trying to see like a scientist, to make notes—again with those words—to keep data, and to make a habit of viewing birds throughout the day, to see them fully by understanding their habitats, feeding patterns, mating, and migration. That sounds like a full-time occupation. I don't think you can see birds this way, but bravo for trying!

Bird Photography

While it's true that taking the picture is more active than looking at pictures in books, essentially you are letting the camera look for you. Then what—you examine the photograph, committing to memory the size, shape, features, and colors? I think we know how that goes. Even as you look, your poor lazy brain will insist "Bird! Bird! I know this one!" and it will offer up what it thinks it knows about birds, instead of actual information about this very bird before you. Furthermore, while taking the picture, you will be preoccupied with lighting, composition, context, and the technical aspects of the camera and lens. All this will distract you from the actual bird.

How to Look

I think you see where this is going: Words are out; photography is out; your eyes, let's face it, in concert with your brain, are just about useless. You're going to have draw birds, if you really want to see them.

NOTE: Cartoon birds are cute; stylized and impressionistic birds show that you know a few things about line, form, and maybe color, but these are more about you and less about birds. You are still not seeing birds. You are representing birds in a way that pleases you.

1. Assemble your supplies:
   —Heavy duty paper that will stand up to erasing
   —A set of pencils in varying tones
   —A variety of erasers, as many as you can find
   —A straightedge and T-square, to help situate your bird in space
2. Find a bird—a really still bird, one that is sleeping or lame. Check wildlife sanctuaries for eagles brain-damaged from eating lead-filled carrion left behind by hunters without dogs.
3. Sit comfortably with your bird. Allow several hours.

NOTE: Your brain, eyes, and memory will try to trick you. Check the lines you make with the lines of the actual bird. Don't be lazy—does the belly really curve that way? No? Erase and try again. Use your pencil to assess the bird's proportions.

TIP: Don't become demoralized. Almost everything you do will be wrong. Don't be afraid to erase. Don't be afraid to start over.

NOTE: When you have the lines right, congratulate yourself on your success. You will now go on to ruin the shading of your bird. Replenish your eraser supply, if necessary.

When You Are Seeing the Bird

You will know you are seeing the bird when you stop seeing its hooked bill, the yellowish cast to the white feathers around its neck, the creepy way it sometimes rocks from side to side while staring vacantly and wide-eyed; you see instead lines and shapes. The bird has vanished, and your brain sees something new. You will feel the shift—neurons firing, adrenaline rushing at this new thing, a network of lines mapping an exotic territory. Your pleasure centers have been activated by the novelty of this encounter, of a magnitude similar to orgasm or the effect of good drugs.

NOTE: The effect is repeatable, by drawing any object—not just birds.

TIP: If you are jaded, tired, depressed, or middle-aged, through drawing you will see—really see—always as if for the first time.

NOTES

1. Herbert S. Zim and Ira N. Gabrielson, *A Guide to the Most Familiar American Birds*. Golden Nature Guide (New York: Golden Press, 1949), 5.

2. Zim and Gabrielson, *A Guide*, 13.

3. Zim and Gabrielson, *A Guide*, 13.

EXILE

Marie Antoinette Escapes to Ireland

The dream: A kid glove, tender white, thrown down a rabbit hole. Mist clings to her cheeks. Clouds roll off the bay, bumping over cliffs. The glove emerges—a key. The key, a man's hand. The doorknob clouds. She rests her head on the wet grass. The clouds roll fast, a carriage to the other coast. Shouts rise behind her. Dew moistens her ear. She digs her fingers into the turf. The glove falls, the clouds race. She wants to let go; she wants to hold on. The clouds' shadows sweep across her—a corset, a wig, a shoe without a buckle—the hand, cleansed of its work.

⸻

Hameau de la Reine

I took the boy to her palace to instill some sense of the world's cruelty. While he went hungry, others had plenty. Rain had washed the blood from the streets, the mobs had dispersed, and nothing had seemed to touch him.

He sat in the shadow cast by the balustrade, knees drawn up, head tucked. Was he tired? Hungry? Finally, he looked up.

Why is the giant sad?

He'd paused by the fountain of Enceladus. Now he wanted an explanation.

The mighty never expect to fall, I said. When they do it pains them very much.

More than it does us, he said.

The pain is the same for everyone.

A look passed across his face—clouds moving fast. I told him about the goats at *le petit hameau*.

It was the queen's special place.

Why are there goats?

Because it pleased the queen.

At the Queen's Hamlet, he became besotted with the goats, murmuring and petting, romping, telling them what fine creatures they were. I waited outside the pen, annoyed by his pleasure. He must have sensed my anger because presently he came to the gate and let himself out.

The queen will be pleased her pets are looked after.

I reminded him that the lady had met her Heavenly Father. He looked up at me.

No, Papa. He placed his small hand on my arm, as if to comfort me. She is in another place.

Which place is that?

She is at home, he said, with her sisters and brothers. They play games and drink cocoa.

And what of the queen's own family?

The boy raised his hand. No, he said, no. He walked ahead, picked up a branch and swatted the long grass beside the path. Soon he grew tired and asked me to carry him.

After supper, to amuse my wife, I asked our son again what had happened to the queen. Still weary from our walk, he yawned and rested his head on his arm.

She sleeps in a fortress on a hill. She will wait until it's safe.

My wife sat very still and said nothing. I wondered how he might further embellish the tale, so I asked him again about the queen's family, her husband the king, their children—A boy about your age, I said, another boy, and a girl.

He sat up, his pale face twisted into a mask of sudden agony, as if he'd been run through with a pike. Breathless from the shock, he sat frozen in that grimace. When he found his breath, the sound that came forth took mine. His mother stood, overturning her chair. I covered my ears. Tears sprang forth as naturally as if I had been wounded. Eventually his mother gathered him to her and took him off to bed.

The next morning, he seemed his usual self. We tended the animals, and he was, as ever, helpful and attentive to the various tasks.

<hr/>

Economy Marie Antoinette

Practicing the economies of revolution, she has her hair done never. The old wig will do. She goes without most days, tucking her formerly regal locks behind her ears, or bundling it into a knot to pick turnips and lettuce for supper. She works the garden in her petticoat and stays—why waste a gown?—and there's no one to do laundry but her. How careless she had been of dripping wax, muddy puddles, the earth in the garden. Now she does her own mending, by candlelight, though this she snuffs to avoid rendering fat. Soap—a luxury. She hoards the hard-milled lavender, inhales its aroma deeply: the last cake, and it would have been gone in half the time if not for her husband's sacrifice. She caught him leaving the cottage that sun-filled morning, having risen in the echo of his footfall on the stair. He stood at the door, rifle cradled in his arm, doorknob in hand. I'll be back, he said. He tipped his head toward the rifle. Dinner, he said. She let him go. In turning on the stair she paused, as if to call out to him. Instead, she stood still, felt light and transparent as an opening between parted curtains.

<hr/>

Monticello

I have ever believed that if there had been no queen, there would have been no revolution.

—Thomas Jefferson

My dear Marie-Thérèse,

I write with news of your playmate and my sweet sister, Polly, who this May found peace with her Heavenly Father and our beloved Mother. Polly spoke of you before her illness, remembering our brief time together in Paris. We mused over Madame Hemings's uncanny sensibility to bring us together—and her cunning at keeping it hidden from Father. Dear Polly spoke of your kindness. She felt, young as she was, an immediate bond with you, though our meetings were brief and too few. I daresay the bond came in part over our dear mothers—ours lost to us, yours so soon to be lost. She raged at the injustice. She argued with Father. The French people, she said, would have found some other spark to ignite their flame. In fact, she never forgave him for his inaction. She called him a coward. I tell you this only to show Polly's depth of feeling for you.

We were in the drawing room, one of the first warm mornings of spring, when the air feels close. Polly was restless, possibly with the onset of illness. She stalked around the room, batting her skirts in an argument with herself. "You could have done something," she said to Father. He looked up from his book. "I could have, yes," he said. She paled, and her lip trembled; this was not the answer she expected—nor I—but he was never one to answer an attack.

"You let a mob destroy them," she said.

Father closed his book. "You can't be certain what transpired. Stories abound."

We had heard them all, my dear—all. I hope you were spared.

I believe she knew the end was near, and she'd made a mental accounting of her life's great affections. We know what it's like to lose family; Polly and I were the last of our siblings. She felt your loss as if it were her own—felt it more keenly for wondering about Father's role. I don't know if she ever reconciled the love she felt for Father and the great affection she felt for you. We had only one conversation after her outburst, the content of which I pore over, but it bears no relevance here.

I wish you would come to Monticello. This fantasy eases my conscience for whatever part my father played in your family's demise. I rest easier simply knowing that you live.

With great affection and humility,

Your own Patsy

Nouvelle-Orléans

Part of the bucket brigade the first time her new city burned, she worked alongside the concertmaster, her old teacher, heaving tarred-leather buckets of water down the line. Inside, the warping wood groaned and snapped, and a terrible caterwauling of flexing strings, bowed by heat, rose up, up—and subsided in the humid night. He didn't have a moment to consider her delicate nature— just felt her there, the motion of her torso, pivoting with each bucket. Music would be made again, he knew, even as the wood burned. Later she confessed that the sound of the city burning reminded her of Paris all that long last summer. It hadn't occurred to her that burning was a way to start anew.

"Paris was not yours to burn," he said. They sipped *poiré* before their pupils arrived.

"Yet it burned," she said. She drank from her small glass and closed her eyes. "I cursed you for stuffing me in that harpsichord. I wet myself."

He began to protest, but she interrupted.

"You punished me. You took me from my family. I rode the street of the condemned. I smelled their blood. I still smell it."

"But not your blood."

"They were screaming—'Burn it!'—because they knew it was mine. I hoped to die. Why didn't they oblige?"

He gave a modest half shrug. "I told them their sons and daughters would play your instruments."

The doorbell sounded with the arrival of her next pupil, the untalented daughter of a well-to-do architect—an ersatz Marie-Thérèse. She opened her eyes and rose. Smoothing her skirts, she strode to the door to answer.

Clio, the Muse of History, Writes Off History

Her docket full with men for centuries, she unrolls the queen's scroll in 1985. Then the washer goes out of balance, her son is expelled from private school, her alma mater taps her for fundraising, and she doesn't resume work until 1998. By then, so much has been recorded, in every medium. She despairs of the task. Instead, she celebrates women with less history.

In the twenty-first century, having caught up on women, she revisits Antoinette's life. She sorts through the intimate moments—private conversations, secret relationships, the girl communing with herself. Some clever humans have imagined for her an inner life, a clandestine life, quite close to the actual: an imaginary figure, yet so thoroughly known. Clio falls asleep at her desk, the cat curled atop the fax machine.

When she wakes, she knows what to do. She buys a pantsuit and chunky heels, revamps her home office, trashes the fax, goes wireless. Her new line: Foresight. She celebrates the unformed; she tells people where to look. From her position, she sees the leggy preteen in Baltimore, walking home from dance class, whispers through her headset into the cerebral cortex, *Prima ballerina, fluent in three languages.* To the boy in Düsseldorf, dismantling his brother's motherboard, *Important inventor.* To the mother in Stockholm, writing a novel while her son naps, *You are a column of fire, searing the conscience of your generation.* At a foreign university, to a so-so student of economics—she finds there are many—*Your country needs you; revolution is coming!*

She finds the sweetly strung-out youngster under a bridge in Paris, his nose bleeding after a light beating. She thinks of her son, what he could have become. *You are a god, my child. Go boldly, shape men!* His smile cracks the blood drying on his face as he feels for the knife in his pocket. *"Shape" in the figurative sense!*— but the timer on the bread machine pierces her consciousness, and she loses the thought. Removing her headset, she sighs and shuffles through the coming month's press releases. Everything has already been written.

Versailles, Indiana

Great-Grand*mare* I calls her, like a big bad dream or a lady horse. I pretend to know more than I know—French and other things besides—but she won't speak anyway, French or German, and she never learnt English. The little girls I've trained to wait on us: Sally makes *petit gâteaux,* each one stranger than the last: lavender-ginger poppyseed; mandarin orange with pomegranate glaze; but Great-*Grandmère* beams at the tower of Lady Baltimore with the glistening butter cream, the white the white of her flesh, powdered smooth in the morning, slick with the glow of her sweat by afternoon. In the garden, she keeps herself covered—big hats and flowing sleeves—but when she bends over, *Mon Dieu!*—the doughy folds, confections of flesh. Polly makes the tea, calls us to table, and the girls serve us in courses: clear soup, cucumber sandwiches, mussels, raspberries and cream, and always the cake, the cake!—the leftovers we find on trays outside our doors at breakfast, sometimes battered and fried, sticky with *caramel*. I taste, I only taste, before I'm off—bathed and dressed to make my rounds. I collect the money that is owed. I see Polly sometimes, through a shop window, pale fingers conjuring an item for her pocket—she never gets caught. Who steals mussels? Everything we know we learnt out of school.

I meet the boys in the park, behind the bushes on the berm. The clouds are pearl-colored, like the pearls in my pocket, Miss Wilson's, the gray like *Grandmère's* eyes. I show them to the boys, Miss Wilson's French still in my ear. Oh, the lessons! The boys adjust their belts and gel their hair, put a shine on their lips and shoes. I show them pictures of the other Versailles, *Not like "sails,"* I tell them, *but "sigh"—what the clientéle do after shaking the bushes.* I have told them of *Grandmère's* many escape attempts. I tell them they will still be my boys in the other Versailles, and we practice our French. I feed them leftover cakes and give them gifts: belts and studded collars, white loafers and tight jeans. We wax each other's bodies clean.

———

Switzerland

To ever be seen through Antoinette's eyes, as one deserving of riches and grace. To be caught in the beam of her approval, which radiates from her being. A cool hand, despite the warmth of her gaze.

"You must stay near to me," she murmurs, pressing my hand to her bosom.

"I will stay close." The doctor's bag clicks shut. She pours me water; the pitcher's spout clinks against the glass. My husband's hushed voice as he confers with the doctor: *strain . . . long journey . . . delirium and fever.* She gathers up her skirts, and sinks down next to me on the bed. I will never again leave her.

"You—" I try to tell my dear Antoinette, but the pain stabs deeper. I gasp. "You are—"

"Yes," she murmurs near my ear.

"You will always be—"

"Yes," she says and kisses my temple, her perfume all around me.

IN THIS LIFE

In this life, John Lennon's parents are American. They don't know John Lennon is John Lennon; he himself doesn't know. He suspects—something. He feels special, then foolish for thinking himself so. At the Amtrak station in New Haven, he waits with his parents for the train to Boston. His mother is a good fifteen years younger than his father. This morning when John Lennon passed his parents' bedroom door he heard a sound—A sob? A gasp?—and paused: and heard nothing more. Now she stands, still and to his left, all three of them staring, silent, at the big board, waiting for his track to be announced.

He could wear contacts, but he likes to remove his glasses when he feels uncomfortable, as he did in the office of Father George, the guidance counselor. The priest revealed John Lennon's IQ. Glancing above his glasses, beyond his desk to John Lennon's foggy form, he pronounced the young man an underachiever. "Not too soon to give a damn, if you have it in you."

John removed his glasses then, and in the soft unreality he thought, Berklee, yes: he saw pages of music on a stand, someone's finger turning them; sitting in the quartet's embrace and waiting for his part to come around in a closet-sized practice room, lost in a world of sound. When he put his glasses on again, he retreated from the hard edges around him, holding himself carefully, away and still, until band practice. He hadn't chosen the French horn any more than he had chosen band. He tested well for music; the shy music director blushed over his talent, taught him extra chords during the guitar unit, and invited him to join band, no audition, at a parent-teacher conference. "I need—the band needs—a French horn; a difficult instrument, but in the right hands. . . ."

Jostling with the other horns, he felt happy and light. Practice alone on the horn felt like the most exquisite kind of loneliness—an extravagant indulgence, to wallow in the feelings of the moment in a self-created miasma or ecstasy. To reunite with his bandmates, to be so vulnerable and alive with them—these were his most intimate moments.

"You look like fucking James Joyce," Tully, the first trumpet, told him.

"James Joyce was an excellent writer," he said.

"It's the glasses," another horn said.

"No," said Tully, "it's the way he looks uncomfortable all the time. Why do you even play that thing?"

"It's as good an instrument as any," John Lennon said, by which he meant I couldn't stop hearing this voice if I tried.

A regretful moment of reflection passed among the brass, most of whom would be graduating soon. What if they had spent the last four years of their lives engaged in activities that, objectively speaking, were no better or worse than others? They had seen this clearly, all of them, and Mrs. B, the music director, watched the pall descend over the horn section, a pall normally associated only with John Lennon, whose name, in this life, is Max—Max Fitzgerald.

Max and his father, who goes by Fitz, came near to having a talk before leaving for the station, while Max sat on his bed, packed and listening: the ticking of the pocket watch given him by his favorite relative, Fitz's delinquent hippie of a sister; the leaves of the maple outside his window rustling in the breeze; the faint peep of small birds; a screaming blue jay; an SUV tossing a low-hanging branch; a child's cry, so rare he thought, "Which bird is that?" What he really waited for: the sound of his own horn, playing a new tune, things he taught himself outside practice and struggled to know. He was waiting to hear his part of "Autumn Leaves" when Fitz caught him.

"I'm proud of you," Fitz said, "and I want you to be happy." What he meant was, "We've invested considerable resources in your development. We expect a return."

Max turned to face his father. "I'll try to do something worthwhile with my life."

Fitz, finding himself annoyed that Max could read him so easily, said, "Atta boy. Let's go. Your mother's in the car."

Max's mother rarely cries, and when she does, the act resembles primal self-protection, the camouflage practiced by vulnerable wildlife: she sits (or stands) still, unblinking, only the faintest hint of trembling. She practiced her camouflage in the passenger seat, staring straight ahead through the windshield, seeing no further than the panic of the one thought in her mind: *If he leaves, I'll die; I'm dying.*

At the train station, she feels fine, relieved, in fact, because she understands now that a transference of power occurs: at the school, Max will become whoever he is supposed to be, and she will have nothing more to do with it. She cannot be blamed for whatever happens next—or can she? She has got him this far without drowning, electrocuting, or losing him to mayhem, never mind kidnappers and molesters, who now seem to lurk around every tree, but who in her girlhood were nearly unheard of. In her day, parents threatened abandonment—at the convent, the orphanage, a midwestern relative's farm. She and Fitz have seen to his education, his diet, his mental well-being, his teeth, his vision (those glasses! Such a handsome boy; why does he hide it?), his hygiene (deodorant, age ten, shaving, age fifteen), his morality, his decency, his respect for elders and the opposite sex, for himself, and for others generally. They've made him understand the value of a dollar without perverting his natural generosity. He's learned Spanish; he likes children well enough. Objectively, well, to her, anyway, he seems OK; more than adequate, well equipped to—what?

Sometimes she has come upon him in his bedroom, cradling the horn, facing the window with his back to the door. She's found watching him a comfort, both of them inert but perhaps communing through stillness. Then Fitz would slam his way into the house and she would slump a little; Max would flinch. Fitz does mysterious things—he lunches with colleagues and golfs with clients. He spends whole weekends at the marina working on his small sailboat, a 1978 Montego, which he lovingly restored. He's schooled Max in sailing and maintaining the boat, which requires constant looking after—scraping, patching, and repainting. Helane wonders that Fitz has not entirely worn the boat away with his attention.

"You have to put the time in," Fitz tells him, often. "There is no substitute for your effort." Max golfs and he is good, a natural in some ways, and his father's friends enjoy his youth and talent because he always loses. His attention often lies elsewhere, though if pressed he could not account for his wandering thoughts. He's not thinking, exactly; he's leaving himself open—for whatever might be interesting. He watches these men, the way they groom so carefully their hair and sideburns, the way they tip the servers in the club, the way they move things forward with each other. How often he has seen at the end of nine or eighteen holes a new scheme hatched, an alliance made. What does Max want? He could never articulate it, or even form the thought, but he can't see how Fitz's friends could connect him to his desires. This golfing and lunch Max understands to be Fitz's campaign; he knows that he should perform his own version of this act in the future. Perhaps he should have been doing so already and has already fallen behind in his accounts.

In the station, while Max and Helane watch the board, Fitz examines the pocket watch. He puts on his spectacles to read the inscriptions—from Fitz's great-grandfather to his grandfather to his father, then, inexplicably, to Fitz's sister, and from her to Max.

Fitz hands the watch back to Max. "In some ways you remind me of Susie."

"Really?" says Max.

"They're nothing alike," Helane says without taking her eyes from the board.

Max wants to know in what ways he resembles his aunt. Is the resemblance auspicious? "I'm thinking of an internship in San Francisco," he says, though he only just thought it the second before he said it.

"An internship," Fitz says. "Smart."

In what, he wonders, as his father must also be wondering.

"Susie would love to see you," Helane says.

Fitz watches the board now, too. "Just don't get lost out there. Your aunt went west with lipstick and a nice smile, and the next time I saw her, she looked like a Boy Scout who ate Twinkies in his tent and read comics under the covers."

Helane smiles faintly. "I don't think that's what she was doing under the covers."

"She had a mustache. She seemed proud of it," Fitz muses.

"All women have mustaches in their natural state."

Fitz laughs. "Nothing natural about living in society, my love."

Helane blushes and looks over Max's head at her husband, and Max feels like an angry child again. Who are these people? He raises the handle of his suitcase, tilting it toward him as if ready to sprint to the track as soon as the ALL ABOARD shows. He's ready, Helane thinks, and so am I. Later that night, after a bottle of their most expensive Bordeaux, she will let Fitz think he has gotten her drunk—maybe she will get drunk—she will fuck his brains out, fall dead asleep, and in the morning cheerfully wave him off to golf, pack her bags, and be off herself. At the bank she will open her own account, take half of what is hers. Her lawyer will deliver the divorce papers at home (eighteen holes, Fitz's ETA 3:00 p.m., post-brunch). Fitz will not be too surprised. A clean break—he'll appreciate that. Their work is done, and once he sorts out logistics, which won't take long—Fitz is fair and efficient—he will search the ranks of eligible lady friends. He will date independently wealthy women. Made as he is for domesticity, he will probably remarry. Helane might not. First on her list, after the divorce is settled: Paris and reading the classics, and anything else good, in French—what she was doing before the interruptions of Fitz and then Max. Though she loves him, Max has truly been the greater disruption. When she thinks of their time together, she thinks of them in the SUV, on their way to Pee-Wee Football, Boy Scouts, the club for swimming, golf, and birthday parties; ski lessons, dances, soccer practice, hockey practice, swim meets, tennis matches, music lessons, tutoring, the doctor, the dentist, the orthodontist, the orthopedist when he broke bones; CYO, Key Club, road races for charity, volunteer work at the animal shelter, various summer jobs, the movies with friends, Christmas shopping, back-to-school shopping, the shore, without Fitz, just to get away. Nearly two decades together, in the quiet climate-controlled interior. They prefer stillness, and that is how she remembers their time together: dazed, tranquil, silent.

Max returns the watch to his pocket, and the weight of it at the top of his thigh, edging into his crotch, thrills him.

"For fuck's sake," Tully said, "a pocket watch?"

Max and Tully were stoned behind the clubhouse one night, after skinny-dipping in the pool. They reclined, still nude, both with raging hard-ons. They thought it the natural state of life. They thought they would always be hard.

"Are you taking it with you to school?" Tully was going to MIT.

"Yes," Max said. "When it breaks, you can fix it." Their hands brushed.

"That watch is the crudest, most depressing representation of time I have ever seen."

"What should I do with it?"

"Give it to your old man."

"He won't take it. Even offering would insult him, like I pity him or something." Max turned on his side to face Tully. "Do you ever think about the future?"

"You asshole—that's all I think about."

"Don't go to school. Let's—"

Tully turned on his side to face Max. "Let's—?"

Max lowered his eyes and dipped his finger into a puddle, dragging it in a looping spiral along the cement.

"You're a good guy, Son of Fitz, but you need to get your head out of your ass."

Max laughed.

"Seriously. What do you want to do?"

Max cradled his head in his arm as he lay on his side and half-shrugged.

"What do you care about?"

"My parents—"

"That's not what I mean, you dope."

Max, high, cracked up.

"What pisses you off?"

"Um . . ." Max said.

"Fuck you and your um. I'm not just some asshole you know."

"You are the Prime Asshole."

"Damn right."

"What pisses you off?" Max asked.

"How stupid and boring almost everyone is. How smug and wasteful we are. We already know about me."

Max closed his eyes. "I just want to lie here. I want to be still."

"How does the world not know what a pussy you are?"

"Maybe I'm Buddhist," Max said.

"You're half-WASP and half-Catholic. I'm afraid to ask, but have you decided on your major?"

"I thought we were high. You sound like my parents."

"You would shit yourself if your parents ever initiated a direct conversation."

Max giggled. "True. Though I feel violated by your question, since you asked, Performance—horn—with a minor in Philosophy."

Tully's silence felt pressurized. "Congratulations. I think it would be impossible to devise a more useless course of study."

Max rolled on his back, convulsed with laughter, his cock slapping his belly. When his laughter subsided, he turned toward his friend again and found them face to face. Tully grabbed a handful of Max's hair. "You can sleep on my couch anytime."

"Your couch," Max said. "I want a wing in your mansion."

Tully released Max's hair and rolled onto his back. Max wanted to know where his people went when they retreated. He wondered if Tully's place was like his, a lake of silence that opened into channels of sound.

He'd been turned on his head ever since meeting with the guidance counselor, that fuck. Tully could never get Max to tell him what the priest had said, but he saw Max go to chapel during lunch for speed-Mass. Tully himself was in AP biology and devoted his half lunch to extra lab work—sustenance and science. He'd thought about cornering the old man, bumping up against him in the hall, pushing him into the lockers and holding him there with his chest. Tully wanted to mishandle him, for Max's sake. What useful earthly guidance could a priest give? Probably this change in demeanor was no one's fault, he knew, maybe just a rattling from surges of hormones, or a flip-out to which the less rational are prone, the fuzzy thinkers, reeling with voluptuous, vague desire for beauty and grandeur, with no way of finding any, lost as they are in the weeds of their longing. Mostly Tully wanted to punch the priest because he found himself thinking, *If only he would apply himself,* which he guessed was what the old fart had told his friend.

Not even Tully knew about the night Max had sneaked out of the house after his parents settled down for the night, his mother to read in bed, his father to do whatever he did in his study. All day, he had successfully evaded everyone: he'd gone to school late, having overslept accidentally. He'd stopped for breakfast at Denny's, where no one paid him any mind, and he engulfed his eggs, bacon, and pancakes. Checking in at the front office before third period, he drew an extravagant signature, which ended in a flourish off the page, about a foot from the face of the secretary. "Someone's got spring fever," she said. "Or senioritis."

"A little of both, I think," Max said.

He slipped into the small space left for him in the regular day. He'd missed religion and biology, the first a dreary subject, as taught by a dour young brother. Max was glad to have missed whatever had gone on; usually he surfaced for questions, none of which he could answer, because they were philosophical tricks, too advanced for Max and his classmates and based as they were on the brother's life experiences. Or they were rhetorical: *Do you think God wants you to have fun?* He was slightly sorry to have missed biology. He imagined Tully calmly conducting the lab, betraying no surprise or concern over his absence. Max was useless in lab. Once, he had shaken a thermometer carelessly and broken it in two; ever since, Tully forbade him touching anything. Mostly he wrote down what Tully told him to, sneaking glances at the pale interior of Tully's wrist as he transferred liquid from one vessel to another.

Between composition and literature, he popped his head into Mrs. B's room to let her know he wouldn't make band practice. "Not feeling well," he said. "Oh, too bad!" she cried. Before she could say more, "Thank you, Mrs. B! I'll see you tomorrow, for sure," and he was off, the fabric of the day torn, himself stepping through.

He turned off his phone. He had no idea what he was doing. The vagueness thrilled him. Key to his enjoyment: the idea that he would go somewhere alone, to have an experience all his own— he'd finally have something to tell Tully. Or, even better, a secret to keep. He stopped at the library and researched bus schedules and downtown jazz clubs. At the park, he practiced his horn and ate falafel from a food truck. At home, he claimed to have a project to complete and begged off dinner. He lay on his bed and listened to the sounds of the neighborhood putting itself to sleep: trash carts rattling to the curb; the clinking leashes of dogs being walked and the soft tones of the humans walking them; crickets; a whoop, from somewhere a scream.

He didn't climb out the window. He left through the side door, from the mudroom. They rarely used the front door, and the back door led to a place outmoded, the place of birthday and pool parties, tucked away now and quaintly remembered like his rocking horse and corduroy overalls. He walked to the bus stop as if it were something he always did, when in fact he had never. He was not sure his parents were aware of bus service. The ride felt comfortable, natural. Mostly he looked out the window, into the dark, and marveled at the landscape, utterly transformed from this new vantage. Occasionally he glanced at fellow passengers, some dozing, some reading or playing on their phones, as if this space were an extension of themselves.

He arrived early at the club, when the musicians were still setting up. They saw him approach the light spilling from the small stage. They saw his youth and his horn case, and they were kind. He explained. "I play, but I don't *play*." He was timid at first, but he didn't panic. He followed and listened for a long time, until he recognized a tune. The saxophonist made space for him, and Max joined in, his horn's voice nasal and melancholy against the saxophone's, which sounded wise and upbeat, taking an interest in him, encouraging him along. Later, he imitated the sax player's more sprightly tones—he didn't know he could do that—and actually felt buoyed by syncopation and time-change. Whenever he knew the tune, he joined in behind the others and thought, this is what it feels like to be a younger brother. At the end of the night his hands trembled from exhaustion or giddiness, he couldn't tell which. The thought that his life could be like this all the time stunned him. Everyone shook his hand and told him to come back. He said he would and never did. When he felt especially down, he remembered. Happiness lay at a club thirty minutes up the road. What would he disturb in going there? He thought about returning the way the depressed think about suicide; he held the moment as a comfort. If he should ever, if things got really bad—but why should he wait until things were bad?

In the train station, he keeps something from himself; it's a little thought, like a worm in his brain, sliding among the crenellations, disappearing around curves, losing itself in shadows of its own creation. Fitz notices his antsy angling with his luggage, and Max sees disapproval. "I can get us some coffee," he offers. In his wallet, he has money—his own, earned caddying; a gift from his aunt, about which his parents know nothing; and a subsidy from Fitz, which he hadn't wanted. *You're doing enough*, he said, but Fitz pushed his hand away, his lips pursed with a disapproval that Max found vague yet encompassing. "Buy a few rounds for your new friends," he said.

Fitz turns everything into a lesson about character. "I don't need any coffee." He rocks back on his heels, as if to emphasize his haleness and lack of need.

"No one needs coffee," Helane says to Fitz. "But," she says, turning to Max, "you should have some if you want it, honey."

Fitz flinches in Max's periphery, and Max wonders if all such partings are so awkward. Fitz follows him to the kiosk at the center of the station. Max has left his suitcase with his mother, but he carries his horn with him.

"Enjoy it while you can," his father says.

The cappuccino machine squeals. "It?" Max replies. He fiddles with some bills, preparing to pay.

Fitz smiles in his habitual, pressed-lip way. "This," he gestures to the horn case, between Max's feet. "Playing at adulthood for the next four years. Enjoy it, because afterwards everything changes—and I mean everything."

Fitz's face reddens as he speaks, and Max wonders if he might be having a heart attack. The idea that his father might do something awkward and unintentional in public interests him. "You mean when I get a job?"

"That, in part. Do you have any idea—"

"No," Max says, cutting him off.

"Well. That's all right. For now."

"You'll meet someone," Fitz continues. "You'll have to give things up."

The coffee arrives in its paper cup. "I don't have anything," Max says. They move away from the coffee stand, and both of them look at Helane.

Fitz nods. "It may seem that way now."

"Am I going to school to get a job and a permanent fuck-buddy?" Max says this automatically; he isn't sure where the words come from.

"I don't think your mother and I would put it that way. But yes, that's what people do."

"What if I don't want that?"

Fitz's laugh surprises him. "Want what you want." He rocks back on his heels. "Don't get me wrong," he says. "You'll like it— sometimes more, sometimes less—working, taking care of your family. It's not bad, not bad at all."

"You're saying all this just happens—it happened to you. You didn't mean it."

"I'm saying there's no choice, son. You may do other things for a while—some do. Don't fight it, is what I'm telling you. The less you struggle, the faster you'll—"

Max doesn't hear the rest. Tully walks into the station; they joked about riding the train together to their separate destinations.

"Excuse me," Max says. He strides over to Tully, who pauses to look at the departures. Tully does not acknowledge him. "Come with me," Max says. "I'm going to San Francisco."

Tully continues to read the board. "What for?"

"I have to get away from this." He waves his hand, gesturing around the station.

"That's why people get on trains," Tully says. "Will you defer?"

"I don't know," Max says. "Maybe. Yes—that's a good idea. I can stay with Aunt Susie, sit in with some bands. Maybe learn about recording."

"What would I do there?"

"Play with me. Go to Stanford. Defer. Anything. Would you look at me?"

"Would I stay with your Aunt Susie, too?"

Max feels he might cry from happiness. Or wet his pants. "Yes, she won't mind—she'd love it."

Tully swallows. Finally, he looks at Max. "You're not going to freak in the middle of this, are you, and leave me stranded in San Francisco?"

Max grabs Tully's wrist, presses his fingers into his pulse. "I would never do that."

"What about your mother?"

"I'll text her. She'll understand."

The big board flashes their track number. Tully shakes hands with Fitz and pecks Helane on the cheek. Max tells his mother he loves her.

"I know you do, honey," Helane says. "And I you."

Max shakes his father's hand and forces himself to look Fitz in the eye. "I'll see you," Max says. Every time I look in the mirror.

Max and Tully walk down the tunnel toward the tracks and wait a suitable amount of time before returning to the lobby to purchase new tickets. Max calls Aunt Susie to announce their plans. On the train, he listens to more of the music he hopes to make, the musicians making worlds of sound together. He watches Tully across from him, who from time to time shows him his research: potential jobs, clubs where they can play, their new neighborhood and life. He's found a studio they could afford, eventually, after they find work, light-filled and near the clubs. Max still feels he might weep or fall to his knees.

"Let's," he says.

The sun leaps into a clearing, catches them both. They squint and shield their eyes.

"Yes," Tully says. "Let's."

HISTORY OF ART

Mars

What he doesn't need: more bronze figures of himself, naked with a spear. Flattering at first, the votives accumulated into a tiny army, ready to wage war for peace, spears hoisted at odd, almost languid angles. He appreciates the nod to his virility—the semi-erect penis, enough to command respect, but modest enough not to detract from the impression of battle-readiness. Some figures arrive intentionally broken, as if they weren't useless enough already, and he arranges the pieces on his shelves. The piles of arrows, swords, and shields please him—he collects for Ares, too, who can't be bothered, so there's quite a hoard. Around supper-time the aroma of burnt offerings—meat, grains, and fish—wafts up to him: delicious foods he can never consume. They won't let him forget what they're up to, the humans. Clinging to their offerings, the faint notion that this war will bring peace.

He prizes most the bronze figures of the devoted themselves, young warriors clothed in armor, a hand extended—a sign that the beseecher would give, however inferior the offering. They remain plump-cheeked and muscular, frozen in their gesture of desire. These beseechers make a separate army, one to whom he owes remembrance. From the corner of his eye at all hours and angles he sees their outstretched arms, palms open to accept their destiny. From time to time he dusts one off, fondly strokes a cheek, recalls the soldier's last conflict. Once and only once did he turn a pair of feet from battle, the warrior confused and melancholy: long life, no glory.

Misdirected offerings tear at him: the bronze eyes and ears, the terra-cotta feet. He'd kept a pair of ears once, longer than seemly, tracing the shell-like curves of their inner workings—as if he could heal or sharpen a perception other than the warlike. Had he prolonged suffering, in keeping devotions not his? His own longing frightened him. He wrapped the ears in linen and delivered them to Our Lady of Perpetual Help. Like an oaf, he didn't say anything, just thrust the package at her. She might have said, I've been expecting these. He fled.

The way he likes himself best: *in silva*, with a colossal scythe, cutting back the wilds for planting. Sometimes, muscles straining, he remembers Ninurta—the god recumbent, wreathed by the fragrance of sesame oil and baking bread—his wisdom that fertile soil needs a fearsome army. The son of Juno swings his scythe, he hacks and hacks, visualizing human crops, rows and rows of sturdy stalks stretching to the horizon.

<hr/>

Londinium

Art is long and so are curses. In the Museum of London, relics of superstitious Romans reside in glass cases that preserve the grudges of yesteryear. The small marble figure of a plump Venus, found buried in the Walbrook Valley; the necklace of emerald beads linked by gold figure eights; the scrap of lead inscribed "Martia Martina."

Your rival scratches your name, "Martia Martina," inverted, on a scrap of lead. She stands at the stream's edge, folds the scrap over, and hurls it into the water for quick delivery to the gods. Later, you stand on the same bank, looking for evidence of your fate in the current. You finger the beads you wear for protection. She dies. You live. You cast a statue of Venus into the stream as thanks for the victory in love. Babies come. You die, of course. And Martia Martina, your backwards name, crackles, metallic, over the speaker system in the museum's permanent exhibition—a curse so old as to make you immortal.

=≡=

Painting as a Pastime

A man needs a hobby to turn his mind from affairs of state. Flowers, for instance, of your own arrangement or en plein air or whatever the staff or the women of the house have assembled or laid carelessly by, such as the bouquet you found under the plane tree at the north end of the heath, tied round with the stem of a daisy. Delighted at first, you thought it left for you by her, but how? She couldn't know you'd come here, and you'd made it clear you wanted to be alone. Still, you set up your easel and spent the afternoon observing: how the center of the bouquet appears crushed, as if a hand, a small hand, had rested on and pressed into it, as if the hand supported the weight of a reclining person. The flowers, the petals, the leaves, bent at various angles, some limp, some—a few daisies—with their heads turned violently, necks snapped. No real care had been taken to create balance. Some flowers were chosen for their proximity to the path: the ethereal and utterly common wild carrot; the equally ubiquitous spear thistle. Yellow goatsbeard, pulled shut now in the midday heat, had lured the rambler off the path, and then she stooped for the red clover, closer to the ground, tiny full globes of itself, like pointillist grapes. In the middle of the bouquet, the stacked faces of the common selfheal glare, dark and lionlike, deep from some damp part of her ramble, possibly near here, possibly the final flower plucked before the gatherer sank to the grass under this tree and care-lessly leaned into the flowers she had just gathered, half-crushing them. And in the grass near the bouquet, a pair of shaded inden-tations, the vague impression of repose. The grass still flattened. You look for signs of recent retreat—a trampled path or bent-back branches—but there's only stillness. The light breeze mov-ing through the leaves and meadow. The wood doves' call. Some buglike chatter. When you turn back to your subject, here and there, the blades of grass have righted themselves.

<hr />

Art Appreciation

The sniper watches as you sketch the beach. Bullets pock the sand around you, sending up small fine showers. Through his sights, he is close enough to see your sketch pad and the hurried way you render the terrain. Men storm the beach; many fall. The only ter-ritory gained will be on paper—a map. He could shoot you, but instead he watches, remembers his first drawing class, years before the world went mad: a vague aroma of pastels and wax; the pro-fessor walking among the students, murmuring corrections here and there. Through the tall windows light streaked in, illuminat-ing dusty air. The still life itself: a goblet with water and seashells; a recently caught fish ("Work quickly," the professor suggested), with its gleaming plump eye; a doll propped on a block of drift-wood, its torso naked, showing where the porcelain limbs and cloth joined; a man's walking stick, broken, an owl carved at its head; a clutch of crumbling dried roses; scattered sand. The pro-fessor's restless energy swirled throughout the room. His magnif-icent sideburns, the one extravagance of his appearance, his droll way of instructing, as if they were all in on the joke—thrilling.

"Forget everything you know," he said, "about seashells and goblets, dolls and fish—if you can forget that smell." The students laughed. "Draw what you see, not what your noodle thinks it knows."

He was an obedient student. He stared and sketched, and as he sketched he felt a shifting in his brain, and then the shattering—he and the objects on the table breaking apart, weightless and drifting. He turned his new eye to the fair-haired girls across the table, their fine features, the jaw, the neck, the collarbones; the professor pacing, the vents in his tweed jacket swinging open; the tall narrow houses adjacent to the school; the canals flowing; the trams creaking; the government buildings with their undulating flags—all a vast blanket of connection. He had never felt such expansive warmth—what he imagined then might be love, or later, simple desire.

He knows you feel the beach this way, to make it just so for the map: no longer *beach* but something strange—not a thing that could be contested, gained or lost. He holds himself very still, his own self shattering with you.

Untitled and unfinished

He was a sentimental painter, his teachers said, years after he'd passed through their classes. No one loved a pastoral more; he couldn't see the point in blowing apart form, or in paint for its own sake. He privileged his point of view and found fault with others'. On cycling trips through the countryside, his stomach growling, the shouts and laughter from the picnics of his youth came back to him. When he walked down the street or smoked in cafés, he saw few faces like his mother's—the blue-eyed, round-faced doll of a woman, so petite and pale. He painted her from memory, placing her amid the settings he loved best: a Bavarian hillside, pausing for a picnic beneath a fir; by the Danube, gazing into her reflection, a castle in the distance; amid a rolling golden wheat field, her silken hair alight around her like a halo. An ideal-ization?—no; a manifestation of her inner beauty, which only he could see. He painted her alone, not with the men who paid her visits, not one of them man enough to pretend interest in him. The settings he culled from memory, of places he'd visited, or seen in books or on other people's postcards tacked to walls. He couldn't ever make her fit, not really—he cursed his lack of talent. The scenes felt static, covered over in a yellowed glaze that sometimes cracked. And she would be there, bent over the gunmetal water as if to do the washing, or slumped against the tree, at rest between chores. Only in the wheat field did her presence make any sense, her illuminated hair rising up to a blue sky, much like the color of her eyes. He'd painted her vest blue, too, the color an accident—too vibrant, he feared, but no; it proved the right exaggeration. It was his last painting. Tired of criticism, he showed it to no one; instead, he translated quaintness of landscape and mother-love to rhetoric and politics. He painted the future with words people could see, like rolling hillsides, and he filled their bellies with echoes of plenty and contentment.

<hr />

LCpl Buckner Visits the National Gallery of Art, Washington, DC

Jackpot—WWI. She thinks I don't know what I'm doing. What did she call me? Peach-fuzz. Peach-fuzz jarine from Virginia. Shit. She's right about the peach fuzz. Go ahead, Peach-fuzz, fight them Iraqis. I need to get with her again, whatever they say. Daddy will send me across the room—Happy landing, motherfucker!—then be done with it. Mama, no. Take it personal, like I can't think of a better way than bring some black girl home. Fucking women. Cold shoulder—ten years? Twenty? Fuck. A gas mask. This shit's weird. That's a urinal—the fuck? Well, a lot of people *did* die. That bastard wishes he did, no-face, in-a-basket mother-fucker the rest of his life, fucking throw me off a bridge. I'd beg Tamika to toss me. Kick me to death with those fuck-me boots, baby. Don't carry me around like no dog in a basket. Fucked *up.* Shit. *What you wanna kill them people for? They ain't done* nothing *to you. You* want *to kill that drill instructor. Kill* that *motherfucker. Seriously.* Those eyes, those lips. Sir, can't go, sir. Girlfriend says I'm a cracker if I do. Sir, yes, sir. A long line of crackers. Breaking the pattern, Sir, yes, sir. These assholes were seriously messed up. Draft-dodger . . . draft-dodger. Figures. Freud-reading officer. *He* can say it's fucked-up—but only after, not during. A long line of crackers, fighting other people's wars. Fuck. She's right. She has the tightest pussy. Nothing, no one—don't think now. Not the time. Ripped-up pieces of shit—train schedules, newspaper. This is art? I'm gonna get shot at for this? Ha, ha. Freedom of speech, freedom, period. Christ, it's my choice. *What you got against them people?* Nothing, all right? Except they have something against me. Us. You think they'd let me fuck your black pussy in Iraq? No? Well, then.

FOREGROUND

She woke up remembering part of a dream, but the dream was real: a memory of Bernard telling her how much he liked to say her name, that it reminded him of the word "alone," that when pronouncing it slowly, one couldn't help but sound beseeching and bereft. "Llloorrrnnaaa," he said, dragging out each sound. As he said it, he reached out to her in slow motion on the bed and then collapsed on her bosom. "Devastating," he said.

The cat eyed her from the foot of the bed. The cathedral bells rang nine o'clock. She'd stayed up too late. She wanted to be ready when Sondra arrived at the gallery; it wouldn't do to have her tell Bernard that Lorna had overslept or appeared in any way negligent, resentful, or unprepared. "Time's up," she said to the cat. She walked in front of the windows without bothering to cover herself; by now the neighbors would have hopped on their bicycles and pedaled off to work or school.

She had stopped bothering with the Dutch newspaper since Bernard had gone. In fact she'd let them pile up on the doorstep until she'd spied a neighbor stacking them neatly to the right of her door. Now, she clicked the television to *BBC World News*. Today in Madrid people were still reeling from the train bombings. Lorna ate yogurt in front of the television, while the cat rubbed his cheek against her ankle. A stock picture of a canal in Amsterdam appeared over the anchor's shoulder. Lorna leaned forward, spoon in mouth. No news about the missing American girl, who had last week waved good-bye to her classmates outside a coffeehouse and hadn't been seen since. No developments, the anchor said. No witnesses, no clues.

"She's covered her trail, Buttons," she told the cat.

Lorna had engineered her own less drastic disappearance eight years ago: a Fulbright and then marriage to Bernard, a Dutch man and nonbeliever, her parents' misgivings remote and weakly transmitted from Ohio. She tried to explain in terms they would understand: a boulder rolled away from the cave of her soul, a rebirth. Now she could disappear for a week without anyone noticing. After two weeks of silence, her father would phone. After two and a half weeks, her mother would call the embassy. She most wanted to retreat to a cave of herself; when she emerged, things would be different, in ways she could not foresee. What she could do with two weeks! What could she do with two weeks?

Reaching into the closet, she disentangled a purple and navy suit from a bouclé dress, yanked the suit free, and slung it to the bed. "Shower time," she said to Buttons, whose ears were back. He gave her a wild-eyed look and switched his ginger tail. The many cardboard boxes, the appearance of his carrier, and Bernard's absence had all raised alarms, and the cat had gone manic—prone to startle and when startled, prone to skitter through the apartment, fishtailing around corners and slamming into walls.

"Don't give me that, please," she said to Buttons. "I can't handle it from you today."

After she showered she tossed the suit to the closet floor and dressed in jeans, boots, and a baggy sweater. At the gallery Bernard preferred her to wear suits and to twist her wavy brown hair into an up-do. Often by the end of the day, Lorna's head ached from all the pins and clips. In the suits she felt like someone else, which was interesting for a while. When she listened to herself speak, half the time she didn't know where the spiel came from. Often, she sounded informed and confident. Sometimes she recognized with pleasure bits of information she'd learned in art history courses and critiques. Always she was aware of Bernard listening. At first she felt proud to command his attention. Later she caught him wincing or frowning at something she'd said, or so she thought; Bernard told her he was too occupied with business to attend to her every utterance.

After she said good-bye to Buttons, she walked along the canal at the street level. A call had come in, and as she walked, she listened to the man on her cell phone, who wanted to buy a painting he'd seen during the last opening, a painting of pig by a Russian artist. Lorna did not want to sell it to him—not for sentimental reasons; she hated the painting. "It's so pink, Buttons," she had told the cat. "It's an insult to pigs."

"It's not that easy," she said into the phone.

"Has it been sold?"

"No."

"Has someone else expressed an interest?"

She said, inventing quickly, "It's a matter of proportion. It's an odd painting, not a very large canvas, and it's all foreground. Are you sure you have the proper place for it? I can't have you taking it home and then deciding it doesn't work over the sofa, if you see what I mean."

The man was talking now, away from the phone, in Dutch. He returned after a moment.

"I assure you, miss, I will not return the painting."

He sounded to Lorna like someone pretending to be earnest in order to get what he wanted. She couldn't be sure. What business was his sense of irony to her? A sale was a sale. They made arrangements to meet at four. By then, Sondra would be at the gallery, having assumed Lorna's role, and Lorna would let her deal with the man.

She pulled open the door to a café; she needed something to steady herself. She sat at the marble counter and ordered coffee and a slice of apple cake. In the mirror behind the counter, she watched a young Korean couple seated at a low table, taking pictures of each other in the weak light. The woman posed with an enormous forkful of pancake poised at her wide-open mouth. Then the woman photographed the man ladling syrup from a crock onto his pancake. Abruptly, they bundled into their puffy coats, wrapped scarves around their heads, and left—their food uneaten.

When she felt a squeeze at her elbow, she expected a tourist wanting her to take a photo, but it was Maarten, the only friend of hers and Bernard's that she would miss.

"Drowning my sorrows," she said.

Maarten sat next to her at the counter, his sandy hair falling across his brow. "In pastry," he said. "A very American mercy killing."

Lorna nodded. "Sweet; a semblance of wholesomeness. I see what you mean."

She had known Maarten before she'd even met Bernard; in fact, it was Maarten who had introduced them. Rather, Bernard had shown up in Maarten's studio when Lorna was helping him print, to complain about the latest increase in gallery rent. It was Lorna who had suggested the move to the canal-level space, to take advantage of a uniquely Dutch situation.

"Must you leave so quickly?" Maarten asked.

Lorna smiled vaguely at his ink-darkened fingernails. She chewed the last bit of cake and wiped the corners of her mouth. "I have no job after today." She'd had to ask her father for plane fare home. Every day between today and the day she left would be full of final moments—her last *appelgebach,* last walk to the gallery, last viewing of *BBC World News* with Buttons, last trip up the cathedral bell tower. The last time she'd see Maarten.

"I'm going to Austria for a month," he said. "My studio will sit empty. Make your art. Don't go home empty-handed."

Her heart fluttered—she loved him for taking her seriously—but she felt a pang at "empty-handed." She'd considered how her

circumstances might be different, had she stayed with Maarten—
not that they'd been a couple; Bernard had moved too swiftly for
that. For a week she had shown up at Maarten's studio at 8:00
a.m. to work, sometimes bearing breakfast; then suddenly she
was waking up in Bernard's bed and falling asleep at night to his
talk about theory. Of Maarten he'd said, "He's a very talented
craftsperson."

"Tempting," she said, and she saw herself working into the evenings, joining Maarten for dinner, the two of them existing peace-
fully in their work and repose. Her face burned, and she looked
down at her plate.

"Won't you feel better, going home with a little momentum?
Take some time for yourself."

"I thought I'd been doing that," she said. "What have I been
doing?"

"You are a lovely person," Maarten said, and Lorna felt the
words like a punch in the gut. She did not feel lovely, and what
good was lovely when you had nothing to show for it?

Outside the coffee shop, Maarten kissed her three times and
slouched off toward his studio. Lorna crossed the street and took
the stone staircase down to the canal level. The gallery was housed
in a cellar, the entrance not three feet from the lip of the canal. She
unlocked the heavy wooden door and shoved until it gave way.
Swollen with moisture, it had become more and more difficult to
open over the years. She had already tidied up the gallery and its
small office. Later, Sondra would swoop in with boxes of promo-
tional materials for the next exhibition; over the next few days, the
paintings would be taken down, and a new show installed. Lorna
flicked on the lights and headed to the office to put away her purse
and coat. She flipped open the date book and recorded the day's
appointment. Maybe she would handle the sale herself—her final
triumph—and go out on a high note.

At the front door, she heard animated Dutch voices. A soft
thudding punctuated the loud chatter; it was Sondra—with

another woman, a customer perhaps—leaning her shoulder into the door. The door gave abruptly, and Sondra and her companion stepped into the gallery, their conversation uninterrupted. Lorna stood in the archway between the two rooms and waited for Sondra to notice her, but she was deeply engaged in describing abstract expressionism, if Lorna understood correctly. The other woman nodded and murmured recognition when Sondra mentioned the CoBrA artists. Lorna noted wryly Sondra's suit and the effect it must have had on her morning: winter-white wool with white fur at the cuffs and collar of the jacket. She must have driven over in that get-up, Lorna thought, which meant harrowing parking, too near the canal for her comfort. She considered retreating into the office and saying nothing. Obviously Sondra knew she was there. If Lorna failed to greet them, Sondra would report to Bernard that she had been cold; if she interrupted to say hello, Sondra might report "sad" or "desperate." She folded her arms and leaned against the doorway, waiting to be acknowledged.

She thought Sondra too old for Bernard, but in fact she and Sondra were the same age. Sondra's energy and efficiency unnerved Lorna. She always had something relevant to say about a painting, an artist, the artist's palette, his or her previous work, a similar exhibition or a write-up she had read. Her wall-to-wall chatter exhausted Lorna, and she felt herself growing sleepy now. She cleared her throat. Sondra continued to talk, while her companion nodded compulsively. Lorna coughed, and Sondra glanced over the customer's shoulder without pausing. Lorna doubled over with a fake sneeze. When she righted herself, rubbing her nose for authenticity's sake, the two women were staring at her.

She saluted them. "*Goedendag!*" she cried.

She introduced herself to the woman, whom she assumed to be a customer, someone Sondra had roped in to see the old show before the new one came in. No doubt she hoped to make some last-minute sales so she could tell Bernard that she'd saved the gallery from the torpor of Lorna's tenure. At the end of the day,

Sondra would clap her hands together, signifying the start of a new era of productivity and energy. Now the corners of her mouth twitched downward. When she caught Lorna's eye, Lorna gestured to the back room.

"Sondra, why don't you make us some coffee?" she said. "There are biscuits, too."

Sondra's neck had begun to redden—splotches here and there, ever-growing continents of color, seeping together to display a mass of embarrassed frustration. She glided away to the back room, neck glowing, to make the coffee.

Lorna began her tour with the pig painting, affecting Sondra-style chatter.

"This painting exemplifies the contemporary Russian take on portraiture."

The woman laughed, so Lorna kept going.

"Think of Rembrandt and Franz Hals: the active gestures, the intimacy of the gaze. Now think of Reynolds and Raeburn: the saucy, impudent looks, the informal poses—people captured in everyday activities. And there's the influence of Millet: common people in their common tasks—the merging of landscape and portrait. All of it here." She gestured to the pig. "Centuries of innovation in painting. The frank gaze—he's really *looking*, don't you feel that? The unusual composition—and of course he's in the barnyard and not elevated or isolated from his milieu. The pig insists on its importance."

The woman smiled warmly and shook her head.

"Do you like it?" Lorna asked.

"No," the woman said. "But your talk is charming." The woman revealed that she was an old friend of Sondra's from school, that she and her husband had just bought their first home in Overvecht and needed a painting for the front room. Something abstract.

"Your own home," Lorna said. "How nice. I'll let you look while I check on Sondra."

Sondra had assembled an attractive tray of three coffee cups and a plate of biscuits. Lorna's throat tightened. "That's really very nice of you, Sondra," she said, "but I've already had my coffee."

Another person wouldn't be so conflicted, she thought, and this was the whole problem—the whole joke of it—the way Bernard said, "Llllooorrrnnnaaaaaa," making an agony of her name. She couldn't even commit to humiliating the woman who would replace her at work and at home.

"I'm glad you're here," she lied. "This is really very nice."

"Yes," Sondra said, lifting the tray, "it certainly is."

The women sat down at a small round table. Lorna vowed to relax. In a week she would be home; she'd made her choices, and those choices had nothing to do with Sondra or even Bernard. Over the phone, her father had cleared his throat and mentioned that the church school needed an art teacher; wouldn't she enjoy that? The job was hers—it was that easy. To be decent in these final moments, in a place she might never see again, would cost her nothing; no doubt she would feel better for having acted properly.

Lorna asked Sondra's friend about her new home: What did it look like? The woman shrugged and shook her head. "Nothing special—typical Dutch."

"I'm sure you'll make it special," Lorna said. They sat in silence, Sondra absently scraping her fingernail against the tabletop. Exasperated by her senseless intrusion—she'd wasted her own time, as much as anyone's—Lorna felt she should finish her coffee, that it would be strange not to. She mentioned the missing American student. Perhaps there had been some development. "So terrible," the friend said. Sondra agreed.

"Maybe it isn't," Lorna said.

Sondra's friend replaced her cup in its saucer. Both waited for Lorna to continue.

"The girl comes to this amazing place, sees things she's never seen. Going home seems impossible, disappointing!" Lorna heard herself talking loudly. Her heart thudded and she forgot to breathe, which made speaking difficult. "So she disappears her old self and starts to make herself over, all new."

The women were silent for a moment. Then Sondra spoke. "If what you say is true," she said, "she deserves to be at the bottom of a canal."

The friend tried to protest, but Sondra interrupted.

"She's rejecting her past, her family, her family's way of life. It's an insult."

"I think it's fanciful, your idea," the friend said. "Like a fairy tale."

Sondra tilted her cup back and downed the rest of her coffee. She took the napkin from her lap and placed it on the table.

"To abandon the people who love her, to cause them such worry and heartache," she shook her head. "And what will she do here?"

The friend smiled faintly. "I'm sure she could amuse herself until her money ran out. It would be an adventure."

Lorna nodded, grateful. "At the very least."

Sondra leaned back in her chair, folding her arms under her bosom. "And after she runs out of money, she can find some Dutch man to support her."

The friend's shoulders twitched slightly. Lorna's face grew hot.

"I see what you mean. Good luck in your new home," she said to the friend.

"It was lovely to meet you," the woman said. "You made me appreciate the pig. I can't say I like it...." she trailed off and laughed a bit.

Lorna gathered her coat and purse. So many things she'd never intended had happened just the same. She didn't think she could justify herself or her actions. At the front of the gallery, on a small side table, she spied a stack of glossy postcards, advertising the current show. She had designed the card on the computer in the back room, with Buttons on her lap. Might as well get rid of them, she thought. Sondra or Bernard would just throw them away.

Typical for March, the sky was a thin gray. A light mist settled itself on the landscape. Utrecht in winter appeared mostly black and white to her eye, with a rich palette of grays in between. In the countryside, from the train window, she saw a different spectrum: browns and the tawny hues of dried grasses, the russet woolly coat of a horse or cow in a field. In the city, though, winter glowed pearly and cool. She ducked into cafés and restaurants, wandered around some of the shops and handed cards to the trickle of tourists and students. She zigzagged across the canal bridges, stopping at a butcher's shop here, a pub there, and eventually made her way to the old city center. She reserved some of the cards to hand out by the cathedral. In the beginning she'd visited almost daily. She'd told herself that the tours helped her learn, and it was true—each time, she picked up a few more Dutch words. On the phone, she could tell her parents truthfully that she went to church nearly every day. Today, as a treat, she would end her last day of work with a trip up the bell tower—all 112 meters of it—for a last look at Utrecht from above, a sight burned in her memory but one that never failed to calm and refresh her. Looking out across the rooftops from far above reminded her how small she was; and what a balm her insignificance was to her. Every building shrank below the tower, and on clear days, she could see Amsterdam and bits of horizon between the buildings.

She stood in the square between the cathedral proper and the bell tower, handing out postcards to anyone who would make eye contact. Tourists gathered to take pictures of the monument to the Dutch killed during the Holocaust—a statue at the center of the courtyard of an angry-looking woman holding aloft a torch. Lorna situated herself nearby, watching the crowd and thinking about packing the remainder of her things. She imagined getting stuck on the bus, sandwiched between her heavy bags, jammed among the commuters. Her heart pounded at the thought of missing her stop, of never extricating herself. Then she saw herself in a classroom: a stick figure clutching safety scissors and a pot of paste, standing before rows of children who awaited her instruction.

In the middle of her reverie, a soft-looking woman with frizzy brown hair approached her. A man Lorna assumed to be the woman's husband followed at her elbow. The woman held a camera, and Lorna readied herself. She held out her hand, her hostess smile plastered on her face.

"I'm sorry to bother you," the woman said in English.

"I'm happy to take your picture." Lorna again felt she was too loud—too something.

The woman ducked her head and patted her hair. "Heavens—I'm a sight."

"You're always a picture," her husband said.

The woman ignored him. "Would you mind," she said to Lorna, "if we took yours?"

Lorna thought she must have misunderstood. "You want to photograph me?"

"Would you mind?" the woman asked again, this time the last word catching in her throat. The man suddenly looked irritable. Lorna wondered about ending up in some tourist's slideshow as an example—of what, she didn't know. "I'm not Dutch," she said, fumbling to understand.

The man and woman exchanged glances. "You remind us of someone," the woman said.

Mist had collected on the man's eyeglasses. "She thinks you look like her sister."

"You do," the woman said, her voice cracking. "Just like her."

An image came to Lorna of her parents, sitting in their kitchen, motionless and waiting for her return. "What happened to her—your sister?"

The woman couldn't answer. Lorna turned to the man, hoping for good news, feeling she was owed it. "Nothing," the man said. "Don't mind her." He turned his wife away and led her across the courtyard, his arm circled around her back. When the woman paused to look at Lorna over her shoulder, Lorna turned away sharply. She strode to the trash barrel and stuffed the rest of the postcards in, sending a few tumbling to the cobbled courtyard. Brushing past the tour group and into the bell tower, she took the stairs two at a time, hoping to wear herself out by the time she'd gotten to the top. She would have her last view of Utrecht, and that would be that.

She paused a third of the way up to peer out a rectangular slot in the thick tower wall. The windows narrowed at their openings, and she felt woozy with the idea of getting stuck. Outside, the statue of the angry woman rose out of the square, and Lorna looked down on her head and the torch she carried. She wondered if the parents of the missing American girl would see their daughter everywhere, always in their peripheral vision, wishing her into existence: at the grocery store or the mall, in their own backyard. For once, she admired her parents' fortitude.

She turned from the window and resumed her rushed climb. The higher she went, the narrower the tower became, until the stairs were too steep and the treads too narrow to accommodate her entire foot. The stairwell was big enough for only one now, and she relished the thought of stomping and raging alone. At the top, she would catch her breath and maybe a glimpse of her own lost self, whoever that was. Maybe she would ask a tourist to snap her picture, to keep as evidence of her once-extraordinary potential in this place so far from the ordinary; maybe she would snatch the first camera she saw and hurl it from the tower.

At the bend in the staircase, a man waited, paused in his descent. Annoyance flashed through her. On second glance, the man looked remarkably like Bernard. Lorna gasped, and tears stung her eyes. An instant later, she realized the man bore no resemblance to Bernard whatsoever. She wondered how far she would have to go to get away from herself. "Could you be less predictable?" she said to herself. "Less tiresome? Please?"

The man must have been waiting for her to pass and she murmured an apology, wiping tears from her face. She proceeded up the stairs, but he didn't move aside. Instead, he raised his hand. She understood, or thought she did, and flattened herself against the wall, her heart pounding. Most people preferred to be passed than to pass, but she had run across the odd person—a man, usually—who preferred to be the passer rather than the passee. Still the man didn't move. Lorna noted his pale complexion and shallow breathing. She had never seen someone get stuck, but she understood the fear. Even people of modest stature had to cant their shoulders, and even so, they were bound to feel the stone walls pressing in on them. She thought she should turn and fetch a guide. Certainly this couldn't be the first time someone had frozen on the stair; the guide would know what to do. Instead, she found herself moving toward the man.

She approached him and turned sideways. "Relax," she said, looking him in the eye. She pressed against him slightly, aware of the edge of the stair, and felt his body go limp against hers. In a panic, she pressed against him more firmly, pinning him to the wall. The man panted, and his hurried breath quickened her pulse.

"You're fine," she said. He stared into her eyes. He was now quite pale—almost gray—and she feared he might collapse if she stepped aside.

"It's okay," she said. "We're not stuck."

He searched her face for meaning. After a moment's hesitation, he glanced over her shoulder and down, down into the center of the stone stairwell. Lorna turned her head carefully, slightly, and followed his gaze. The stairwell was more capacious than she'd remembered. In fact, if she lost her footing, she could easily tumble down the one hundred or so meters, with time enough to think things through—how stupid it was to fall, how careless; how idiotic to think she could get stuck; how incredulous her parents would be to lose her like this, so near her homecoming, after having lost her, temporarily, once before—shattering various body parts along the way on the long trip to the first story's stone floor. Survival did not guarantee recovery. She pressed harder into the man. "Don't," she said. "We'll fall."

FINE ARTS

The affair was necessary. The thought comes to you in your small town's small art museum. You stand before the horse made from aluminum soda cans. Your daughter holds your hand, tugging and pitching like a kite caught in the wind. She has seen the horse before; she knows her business here, and it involves crayons and low tables and other children, in a part of the museum where talking and touching are permitted. An older couple pauses by the sculpture. You wonder if the white-haired woman in the coral jacket would understand your affair. Does she keep secrets from her husband? What kind? How many? The unbidden attraction to a stranger, the price of a pair of sandals? Does she think about confessing? The two of them are uniformly brown and wrinkled, as if they have sat on the same beaches, roasted on the same shores, every minute of their lives.

From behind, you feel the hot push of humid air on your neck and bare arms; your husband and son approach from outdoors. They join you beside the horse sculpture. Your husband nickers and whinnies softly. Your son, his eyes shining with admiration, pulls on your husband's lips. He watches carefully to see how this new sound is made. Everything you do amazes the children now, though you know that soon—in a few years—all your jokes and habits will have worn irritating grooves in their brains.

In the rotunda, a plaster statue of a woman commands the

entire space, though she occupies only a tiny portion at the center. Her top half is curvy, slope-shouldered, with perfect apple breasts. Her lower half is gryphonlike; in one clawed foot she holds a small globe. Her wings would seem to beat the air, but the coils of her hair stand away from her head and suggest falling. Her plaster hair is painted yellow and her wide eyes are green, her parted lips pink, plump, resigned. She's falling, and she's taking the world with her.

"She scares me," your husband says.

You wonder if she was modeled after the artist's wife or girlfriend. "You should be scared," you say.

He doesn't mind art, your husband, and that bothers you. You doubt he's ever been seriously troubled by it. You wish the artist had painted the falling woman's nipples, or put a ring through one of them.

He doesn't mind art, so he'll take the children to the activity center, where volunteers hand out vinyl bags with paper and crayons. He doesn't mind the coloring, or the time spent with the children. He is happy to give you this break. He knows you'll return refreshed, that you'll squeeze his arm on the way out and regard him with flustered gratitude. He'll draw you a picture at the small table with the children—probably a heart or a bicycle. He's very good at hearts and bicycles. His hearts are anatomically correct and sometimes festooned with garlands of flowers, or superimposed with maps—the place where you live marked with an alligator on the blue-and-red highway of the descending coronary artery. It's the one thing about him that surprises you still.

You enter an exhibit of twentieth-century cityscapes in black-and-white, and your world falls away. For the time you spend in the exhibit, the world of the photographs—the grit of the sidewalks, the damp of the air—is more real to you than your world. You peer into the lighted blocks of tenement windows, trying to glimpse the lives inside. What did they care about? Whom did they love? In one image, the uniform blackness of the night provokes a longing in you to plant your thumb in the sky, to leave a dull smudge.

You amble through a temporary exhibit of Asian sculpture. Diminutive warriors hold phantom shields and spears. You're sorry about their missing noses. Some have lost fingers, unable to let go of their gear. The statues have value for the simple fact of their longevity. Hang in there, they seem to say, you may lose only your nose. You touch the finger-stubs of one warrior and feel awe for the missing pieces; in their absence they grant this body more power. You think of the gryphon-woman, her falling-yet-clutching, her wild tenacity. How thrilling to persist, to fall, to lose.

You find your way to a low chair set before a window, overlooking a small courtyard. Lizards scuttle over small stones, plunging into the tangle of vines and palmettos. You ease into the low chair. There's something about this position—knees higher than hips—that soothes. Your husband told you once, something to do with blood flow. "Or maybe you just like it," he'd said, careful to avoid reducing your every preference to biology, though you're not sure you mind biological explanations. It's another bit of solicitude on his part, and you wonder how much of his brain he devotes to thinking about your concerns. Perhaps today, as a tribute to your wedding anniversary, he will draw a picture of his brain and mark all of its centers that are consumed with thoughts of you, though he would qualify the implication of "centers": "There's no single place where thoughts live," he has said, "only pathways, reinforced by rehearsal."

As you watch the lizards, you think about the art in the museum where the affair started, in the city where your husband conducted his residency. While he saved people or didn't, you tended your affair. Frank Stella—his prints, not the man—started it all. The set of five prints possessed an unmistakable eroticism, though there wasn't a curved line among them. You had always thought of the erotic as a curve.

In the Museum of Fine Arts, for all your posturing about your love of abstraction, what you really loved was its apparent meaninglessness. You felt the prints; you didn't think about them. For the same reason, the nineteenth-century sculpture did you in, the semiclad females—a breast perched above the fold of a tunic, a toe peeking out of a sandal, the placid lips that would always keep secrets, the stolid gaze implying there were secrets to be kept. In this state—your mind free of reason, your breast longing to be exposed—the affair seemed inevitable. You could tell your husband, persuade him it was necessary—that your cells cried out for it, for where was he? Becoming a doctor. Becoming the man who would support your family, who would draw pictures with your children while you try to justify an affair of many years past.

In the gift shop, you purchase a postcard and address it to your former lover. Every year you send a different card. This year it's a postcard of the gryphon-woman. You never write a message. You imagine he smiles—a twitch at one corner of his mouth. Maybe he saves the cards, maybe he doesn't. This year, you want to buy two cards. You want to find exactly the right image for your husband. If only you could send him the quiet face of the marble beauty in Boston. Here there's only the wild-haired, wild-eyed falling woman. You settle finally on a postcard depicting an off-white piece of paper that has been folded and unfolded. The creases have been printed with white ink. You write, "The affair was necessary." You know this is true, and not true. Too much has been made of this. You address the card to yourself.

Back at the activity center, you admire your children's drawings of the falling woman. Your son has colored her lips green. Your daughter has given the woman a daisy tattoo on her left breast. Your husband has drawn two hearts. The hearts are side by side, almost touching but not quite. He has drawn them carefully, from the crown of pale arteries to the glistening shroud of the pericardial sac. He has labeled them: "Mine" and "Yours." Yours is the larger of the two.

THE WAR ARTIST MAKES GOD VISIBLE

AFTER STANLEY SPENCER'S GREAT WAR MEMORIAL

Resurrection 1

The captain holds his helmet. Four bayonets pierce his torso. Ferns grow from his wounds. He knows the body rejuvenates; he's seen it in the wards—the growth of new tissue, the expulsion through the skin of glass shards and shrapnel. While he stands holding his helmet, watching his men touch their wounds and feel warmth returning to their limbs, his own veins burn and thrum with the fire of blood. What could God mean? He imagines the vicar clearing his throat, fumbling for the bottle of scotch he keeps in his file cabinet, behind the records of births, weddings, and deaths.

The captain regards his ferns with tenderness. Mature leaves fan from his various wounds, and bright-green fiddleheads push their way through the bubble of his newly coursing fluids. On his walks at home, he had admired the lushness of ferns, the plant's ability to flourish between the cracks in stone walls.

<hr/>

Resurrection 2

If any believed in such things, not one thought his resurrection would return him to the trenches. The soldiers gaze around them, reaching for their gear. They confirm their experience in each other's eyes.

One man leans against the trench wall, his face half-buried in the crook of his arm. He stares through the tangle of barbed wire. The earth is dry as ever. He imagines riding a train home to Cookham, embracing his mother and his sister, their smooth cheeks and nice-smelling hair. And his girl who can't refuse him now—having been dead and come back raises one up in more than one sense. He imagines the girl waiting at Victoria Station. He will see her before she sees him, and it will seem to take forever to walk across the station. She turns her perfect face to him, and in that instant, he tastes meat pies and cider. A musty smell fills his nostrils, of the tiny paperboard houses and cotton-wool hedges that will make up the miniature town beneath their Christmas tree. He'll say, "I've died and come back. I've *died*." She'll think he's mad. She'll expect him to get on with things—find a job, earn his pay, support the family they will have.

He opens his eyes and turns toward the trench to face his mates, who fasten their belts and holsters. He catches the eye of one. "This is a fright, eh, mate?" The other man laughs and shakes his head. His face is stone white and still tinged blue around the eyes. "Never telling anyone this."

He closes his eyes again. Somewhere down the line, a flag snaps in the wind. In a moment the captain will pat his shoulder and hand the soldier his gun.

———

Resurrection 3

The dead and the wounded lie on stretchers pulled by mules and are bathed in the glow of the dressing station. Inside, white-draped figures tend to the wounded man. Despite the shells and gunfire, the mules stand calmly, gazing at the lantern-lit scene. A soldier leans against the corner of the building and peers in. One stretcher-bearer, loath to leave, looks to the soldier he has just carried, even while he turns toward the front, toward the bodies he has yet to collect. He cups the soldier's cheek in his palm.

≡

Resurrection 4

The lunatics are good workers.

> —Stanley Spencer, writing from Beaufort Military
> Hospital, Bristol, 1915

Iodine of jam on stairsteps of bread heavenward. Urns of milky tea. More than enough of this and only this for everyone on Earth. Every part must be saved for the day peace comes. Little slivers of soul scraped from the feet, the rotted black bits and scooped-out divots, the legs and arms I will keep safe until the time when all are made whole again. Every corner scrubbed, all stink washed away. The sack stinks. My burden. The little fellow, he records the soul of each man, gives the drawing to him for the day our Maker sends his Son. Each has a record of his sacred soul. We are Christ's angels, disguised here on Earth as we are.

Ever busy, Sister Mother says, ever at rest—though never to me, only to the little fellow, who hides in the bottom of the linens closet with his books. We scrub floors together, he and I, though we know our work is more than it seems.

Every precious soul preserved, but I ask and ask about the souls still abroad. They lie where they fall, the captain says, along with my eye. I change his bandage at night, when Sister Mother sleeps, the eyehole covered over with wrinkles of skin.

I'll go with you, I tell him. We'll find the rest of your mortal soul and all the others, too.

How will we ever find that? he asks.

We'll comb the earth, I tell him. I wrap his filthy bandage around my hand. If ever it existed we will find it.

Resurrection 5

The soldiers struggle to rise, entwined as they are in their white picket crosses. Already their capes make wings. "Spencer would make us all angels," one grunts as he hoists himself out of his grave.

The others groan, cursing, and struggle to extricate themselves from similar holes. One stares down at his tunic of feathers, worrying what the others will think. What sort of man picks around the battlefield like a half-plucked chick? Others reach out their stone-white arms to each other, without thinking; in the grip of such embraces, there's no turning back, and what does this make them? Here on earth again, locked in each other's eyes and embraces, grown men, stone men, stiff-upper-lip men, with a feeling that itches up their palms and forearms as they clasp hands. The itch crawls across their biceps and burrows into their armpits. It shoots up the backs of their necks and creeps along their scalps, follicle by follicle. The itch burns permanent pathways in their skin. The feeling is almost like love. It will have to be satisfied.

REPATRIATION

I

The morning of the funeral, target practice with her brothers in the backyard, the nearest neighbor too far off to be bothered. The old man had saved Schweppes cans—had been saving it looked like years: bushel baskets and peach crates filled with them in the dank barn. On arrival, they fell to cleaning, not that the rifles needed it. She had mixed a pitcher of Manhattans—his favorite, a bilious-looking drink—and poured them into insulated plastic tumblers, cracked and glittery relics of their 1970s-spangled childhood. They took turns picking off cans. After the Manhattans were gone, she went back into the house for the shotguns. In the early-morning gloom, she stiff-legged around, kicking over the embroidered footstool, bashing into the lamp table, sending his crossword dictionary slapping to the floor. She heaved his 12-gauge out of the safe and found her brothers' too. She cradled them in her arms, a bouquet, stumbling and sliding her way across the wet grass toward her brothers, who had put down their guns and were drinking beer now.

"You look like a different ending for *Carrie*," Bell said. "Why don't you fetch another round?"

"Because she wants to *shoot*," said Clayton.

"Damn straight. Fetch it yourself," she said to Bell.

He sat in a plastic lawn chair beside a plaster statue of a

squirrel. He tapped its head with his forefinger. "Do you think he meant to tell us?"

Clayton handed her shells. "If he'd wanted us to know, we'd have known he was dying before he turned up dead."

"Toss a can, Clayton." She raised the barrel, and Clayton pushed it down again.

"Let's not."

"I want to," she said.

"Punch my chest," he said, puffing himself into a broader target. "Punch me."

He wavered, his blue dress shirt aglow, the outline of his white T-shirt stark at the neck. She unloaded, set the gun down. "I could break something," she said.

Clayton handed her a beer. "You could at that."

II

Later, post-funeral and after the folk cleared out, they were left with food and liquor enough for four Christmases. The house he'd left clean and spare. They found nothing more personal than what appeared to be toast crumbs from his final breakfast scattered on the kitchen counter. In his will, their father had stipulated that the house and land be sold, the proceeds shared equally among them. His art books, slides, lecture notes, and other academic papers he had already donated to the library of his alma mater. On the subject of the marble bust, the will remained silent; it was simply gone. She thought the boys must not know about the head, as she'd come to think of it, which had sat in her father's closet, pale and glowing, since she was a girl—probably longer. She had known on instinct that it had come from the war. Most fathers kept enemy bayonets or Nazi flags, but hers took a souvenir more suitable to his line of work.

The bust first appeared to her shortly after her mother's death. In those first few days she wandered the house, unmoored and unsure what to do with herself. Meals appeared sporadically, left on the counters by neighbors or pulled by her father, charred and smoking, from the oven. The boys had gone into the woods, hunting; she was too young for that. She'd been avoiding her father, making herself small and darting from rooms before he entered, his sorrow an animal slinking ahead of him. She came across him by accident once, while he stood in front of his open closet. She crept up behind without his noticing and saw what he saw: the pale glow of the thin-faced woman nestled among his silk ties on the shelf. Thick plaits of marble hair framed her face. Part of her upper lip and nose had chipped away, and the image flashed in her girlish mind of a roller-skating accident—the stone woman teetering, falling, her face breaking on the sidewalk. Later in adolescence, gasping in bed at night, she imagined the woman shattered by lust and rough kisses. The bust's appearance, she knew, had something to do with her mother.

When her father opened or closed the closet door, the hinges, smothered in decades of paint, moaned and squeaked. In the early days when she heard the sound, her heart jolted, electrified. Later the sound wore on her—a grating down her spine so real she sat up and shivered. Eventually she heard the sound even when he wasn't home. It distracted her from homework and chores. She took to visiting the bust when he was at the university or running errands. She touched the cool marble with her fingertips, traced the broken nose and blank eyes, pinched the chin between thumb and fingers as if to snap it off. Once, she slapped the cheek. The bust stared, placid and remote.

She began painting her own face lavishly with makeup, chopping her hair and dyeing it lurid colors. Her father regarded her with surprise and possibly offense, as if to say, Who are you? Mine? I don't think so. Then she stopped eating, which landed her in the hospital, and she was as inscrutable to him as ever. Clayton and Bell tended to her, in their offhand way. So casual was their method that she was never sure they actually cared for her; they seemed to find lounging by her railed bed fine for talking about baseball, hunting, and girls. She fed off their attention. Back at school, she enveloped herself in a shimmering veneer of functionality—extra effort in all things, from grooming and studying to volunteering at the nursing home and singing in the church choir; excellent grades; the acquisition of friends and languages—her drive emanating from a hardened core of spite. She was too busy for her father. She didn't see him to know if he was looking. In the end, they had the same head after all, for art and quiet study. She did not think her activities bore any relation to him.

III

She found a real estate agent to list the house and farm. At home, she could not forget the bust. From her research she learned it had likely been commissioned by a wealthy Roman in remembrance of his dead wife. Occasionally the bust appeared to her in the middle of things—unloading the children from the car; staring over a glass of wine after dinner; during faculty meetings, her face masked with contemplation. She imagined different fates: What if her father had donated it to the local museum? He'd have to answer for having it, though a dying man might not care. She pictured the head in a landfill, a banana peel draped across its ruined nose, or planted in someone's yard in town, next to a gnome or bonneted goose, by the koi pond or in the birdbath.

She found herself unable to comprehend why he'd stolen it—a complete perversion of the task he'd been assigned. After the war, Europe was a ruin of obliterated places, people, and families. Perhaps in that chaos, he felt the bust belonged as much to him as anyone. Who, after all, would give it such attention? Maybe he'd tried, later in life, to ship her back to her place of origin, but surely that place no longer existed. Maybe he'd waited for someone to come looking.

The land sold quickly, for commercial development, the house to be torn down. In her mind she revisited every room, opened all the closets and cupboards. She imagined her own ghost in the future, haunting the inevitable strip mall that would occupy the spot where she'd grown up.

IV

She recalled a museum visit she and her father had taken together, when she'd returned home for winter break. The museum had emptied its storage facility and put on display every antiquity in its collection. She paused before one of the many glass cases, stunned by the sheer number of lead spoons, foggy glass vials, iron hairpins and makeup spatulas—millennia of refuse, lost or abandoned by humans as they pursued and fled one another across the globe.

"Does this make you love or hate humanity more?" her father had asked.

"I feel sick," she said. "People owned these things, and now they're dead."

"Yes," he said, "they're so dead they're not even dust. So, you're undecided?"

She'd passed around his back to view the terra-cotta canopic jars. Jackal-headed lids protected the ancient innards of wealthy Egyptians.

"Those dummies," her father said, following her gaze.

She would have felt stunned, had she not already felt stunned. "I didn't know the Egyptians were dummies," she said. "They're not generally known for that."

"They certainly thought a lot of their spleens," he said.

"They didn't know any better."

"Exactly."

She felt stung, as if she had been tricked. Was this the same man who had adored a representation of his dead wife? She itched to slap his face with his own sentimentality, but she felt foolish—ignorant of some great and sneering knowledge he possessed.

Months passed at school, her feelings smothered by the academic calendar, exams, reading. At night, as a comfort before she slept, she recalled images of the famous artworks she studied, and often she dreamt of them. There they were, night after night, familiar and unchanging in their details. Except that, years later, when she became fortunate enough to view the works themselves, it was as if she were meeting an old friend for whom she'd once had warm feelings, feelings that brimmed to the surface, only to find that no such feelings existed—the friend a stranger. Something in her memory had altered the images—her mind had intensified focus on some trivial aspect of a painting, or misremembered the position or demeanor of a figure. On her honeymoon trip to London, in the National Portrait Gallery, she'd left her husband frozen in distress as she searched for her favorite Reynolds, which clearly hung on the wall before her. Over and over, she compared the title next to the painting with the title she'd written in her small notebook: they were the same, but this was not the figure of her memory. She accosted a docent, pointing to the title written in her own hand. "Where is this painting?" The docent, an elderly woman, clutched her arm and said, "I'll fetch someone. We'll get it sorted," and never returned. She felt the loss as she would the death of a friend. She became timid of her memory and began to suspect she might have fabricated the exchange she'd had in the museum with her father.

V

Sometimes she thought to mention it—all of it—to her husband: the missing bust, her father's misanthropy, her jealousy aroused by an object. Then she thought, for God's sake, it's a thing. The bust had stood for someone real, though, and people had stood before it in memory of that person. They were all dead now, including her father. She broached the subject instead with Clayton, in a late-night phone call, both of them outdoors, a thousand miles apart and hiding smokes from their spouses.

"What did you think of Dad's war booty?"

Clayton exhaled. "Got no idea what you're talking about."

"The bust—the head—of the woman?"

"He had a woman's head?"

"A portrait bust." She leaned on the deck's railing, moving only to guide her cigarette the short distance to her mouth.

"I don't recall any such thing. He brought this home with him? How?"

"He probably shipped it to his university. He kept it in his bedroom closet, with his ties."

"Whoa—what are you smoking?"

"What are you smoking?"

"There was no head in Dad's closet. Maybe a hat form—is that what you saw?"

"I touched it. I slapped its face. It was marble—"

"You slapped it? OK. I believe you. No, I never saw it."

They smoked quietly and said nothing for a while.

"Why would he take it, though?"

"You want this to make sense?"

It had never occurred to her that a logical reason couldn't be found.

"Well," Clayton said, "anyway, there's nothing left, so just forget about it."

But there were hairpins still, and Schweppes cans and rifles. Maybe he'd been right to get rid of things. She'd told her brothers to do something with the rifles and shotguns; he must have forgotten them, or maybe he hadn't. She couldn't guess his motives. He had been for so long the man who had stolen something beautiful, broken, and human, obsessed over it in secret, then disposed of it. She wondered who he'd been before he went to Europe. She wished she had some memory of his potential to embellish, a version of *father* to suit her needs.

CHINESE OPERA

I kept the guts of the music box after Donny smashed it. The black lacquered wood had shattered on the staircase while in his crib our son shrieked his face into a purple mask. My father had given me the music box as a reward for singing at his boss's party. At the party, he took me aside—into the bedroom of the boss's daughter. Her white-canopied bed glowed, the dust ruffle a cloud. He leaned down to speak to me.

"I want you to do this," he said. Light from the vanity lamp reflected off the thick lenses of his glasses, so that his eyes were a blurry glare. "I really, really do."

I shook my head and shrank into myself. Pressing me would cause more resistance, he knew, and he straightened. He glanced at the music box on the antiqued dresser, and my gaze followed his. The lid was open to display a figure from the Chinese opera. Her face was pale, her cheeks painted in swaths of begonia pink. Over her head she brandished a silver sword, and two feather plumes rose from her black hair, like the wild curling horns of a ram. Her chin pointed upward, her face lifted in righteous fury. The angle of her left arm suggested a foe advancing from beyond the velvet lining of the box, one she was prepared to smite. I hung on the force of that gesture. My father saw my need.

"You like that?" He reached for the music box. My heart fluttered at the thought of his fingerprints marring its glossy surface. "I'll give it to you."

My breath caught. He nodded. I felt smaller, but hard and sharp, gathered together in some vital way.

I sang in a corner of the kitchen, the adults standing around me, attentive and straining to hear my voice. In the car on the way home, my father presented me with the music box. I don't know how he smuggled it out. A few months later he overwound it. The figure remained stuck with her sword down, her white face and painted-on eyebrows directed abstractly at the objects I'd collected: a four-leaf clover; a wooden nickel tossed from a parade float; a plastic ballerina I'd swiped from a friend's birthday cake, hardened frosting still clinging to her pointed foot; one wheatback penny.

Then Donny got his hands on it. The barrel and tines look like 10-karat gold, but they aren't gold. I don't know what they're made of.

GIRLS COME CALLING

Every day between four and five, my old friend took a nap. He refused to lock his front door, and a gang of wild-haired girls from the public school would let themselves in shortly after four. They had claimed his corner as their territory and the summer before had spray-painted a pink death's head on the sidewalk in front of his house. I imagined them escaping the heat of late afternoon, their dusky faces poised in the cool dim hallway.

The first time it happened, the girls wrote messages on the inside of the door in pink lip gloss and purple nail polish. Afterwards, I stood looking with him. I'd come over to borrow a book. Lately I'd made it a habit to feign some need in order to check on him. I often found him sitting still, a cat curled in his lap, papers and books piled on the table in front of him. He looked, in these moments, as if he were reading from a great distance.

"You should lock your door," I said.

"You can tell a lot about the culture this way," he said, gesturing to the door.

I thought I should know what he meant, so I didn't ask what he saw. The girls had written vows to their best friends and unkind descriptions of girls they did not like. They made their signs, flowers with bubble-like petals, skulls clutching rosebuds in their sardonic mouths, cartoonish smiling horses and cats. He didn't repaint the door, and for a few days the girls added to it with spray paint, bits of broken mirror, colored buttons, bottle caps, and tissue paper, until the door glowed and shimmered with color. None of the original paint showed. The girls made a border of feathers around the doorframe, a single row alternating hot pink and orange. He said it took them a week to complete, and sometimes he woke to hear them talking as they worked. I'd assumed he slept straight through.

"Why don't you call the police?" I said, and he said that the sound of their industry never failed to put him to sleep again.

When the girls finished the door, they started other small projects. They cut out a cube of space from the pages of *The Riverside Shakespeare* and constructed a tableau in the shadow box they'd created. They used fabric from my friend's old button-downs and gardening pants to make rolling hillsides, trees, and honeysuckle vines. They whittled tiny girl-figures from clothespins. All the girl-figures held hands, and they wore their yarn hair in pigtails tied with colorful bits of rag.

"Why'd they choose *The Riverside Shakespeare*?" I was wondering about the cultural significance.

My friend wheezed in a way that sounded profoundly meditative. "It's the right size," he said.

Over time the girls' efforts became more grand. During the summer, they entered a phase of bringing the outdoors in. Over the back porch stood a wisteria-draped arbor that filtered the light to hazy lavender. The smell from those velvety bunches was lovely, but it was too hot to sit outside—the heat made my friend's legs swell—and the mosquitoes were ferocious. For two weeks the girls disassembled the arbor and reassembled it in the living room. They devised a system of troughs in which to transplant the wisteria. My friend thought to take longer naps in order to give them more time for their labors, but he feared insulting them by suggesting that they needed the time. On the last day, they strung white lights through the vines to mimic the stars, which of course was pure fancy; we were too close to the city to see stars.

For a while the girls went into a fallow period, which my friend said was necessary for creative types. He woke to the smell of popcorn and found an oily bowl with a few kernels unpopped at the bottom. He'd find his books on the coffee table, tented or with pages dog-eared. The girls were reading Chekhov, Kafka, Woolf, and Dave Barry. They added items to his grocery list, and dutifully he purchased these: chocolate milk, peanut butter, marshmallow fluff. In the evenings we sat in his new living room, drinking chocolate milk and gazing at the girl-made heavens. He said he'd heard them talking about the ceiling, how to paint the sky in the exact way it appeared at the onset of dusk, when parts of it seem drained of color. Their voices, he said, were full of awe. They decided not to attempt it.

Books he'd never seen before started showing up—untranslated Rilke—and sometimes he heard them practice their German. His eyes shone with pride when he told me. I picked a kernel of popcorn from between the couch cushions and popped it in my mouth. "Well," I said. "Good for them."

In the fall school started, and as far as he could tell, the girls slept. They came—he could tell by the disarrangement of the couch pillows, the way every item in the room appeared slightly askew: magazines hanging off the coffee table, about to drop; the remote control slipped between the cushions; one crumpled white sock beneath the kitchen table. The cats looked more dazed than usual. They lay draped across the couch and armchair, their narrow bodies exhausted from so much petting, neck-ruffing, and cheek stroking. The fur around their eyes and forehead had been rubbed the wrong way, and they squinted and purred their besotted approval at us.

The days became crisp, but the girls didn't. My friend still woke up—from their silence, not their voices. Occasionally he heard a plaintive syllable or sigh, the rustling of a page or skirt, but nothing more.

Evidence of boys appeared. Different, deeper voices floated to his room, their laughter squeezing his heart into a crazy thumping.

"Young love," he drawled one day when I started up from the couch.

"Wet spot!" I cried.

The boys left a musty funk—an unfresh quality covered over with unsubtle cologne.

"They stink," I said, flapping an issue of *The New Yorker*.

"The wisteria's dead," he said. Spots had formed on the twisting trunks, and the leafless mottled vines seemed grasping—bounded by the walls and ceiling of the living room.

"And they're rude." One or several boys had written a series of limericks about my friend's ancestors and had tacked them on Post-its to each sepia portrait. The little poems were formally correct, and I suspect the girls were impressed. My friend delighted in the boys' verse, chuckling and finally wheezing until his face went pure red.

"The boys don't hurt anything," he said, smiling fondly. "They just eat a lot."

"Still," I said, "the girls have been fallow a long time."

"True," he said. "They are distracted."

"Lock your door," I said.

He held up a white footie sock, which he had retrieved from beneath the coffee table, as if it explained his position. "I can't," he said, shaking the sock at me. "I won't."

I came over last week to find him still in bed. The cats sat high on the top shelves of bookcases, squinting and switching their tails. The girls stood all around his bed. One sat in a straight-back chair beside him, holding his long-fingered hand. Another smoothed the hair away from his forehead. Already the color had drained away, and one of the girls remarked upon the alabaster cast of his skin. In the living room, the boys waited on the couch, reading magazines and doing their Latin homework.

THREE PORTRAITS OF
ELAINE SHAPIRO

I

Elaine Shapiro visited New York City for the last time when she was twenty-two. She rode in from New Jersey with her boyfriend Avi at the wheel to attend the wedding of his cousin, a bronzed blonde with line-thin brows. Elaine had seen pictures of her at the shower: riding horses with her fiancé, sunning herself in a bikini on a cruise, posing with sorority sisters at a fundraiser. She had just found a job in publishing. "Not a job," Avi had said. "An internship."

Avi and Elaine were supposed to be married. They had met at a JCC dance after Avi's first summer in Israel. Elaine thought he resembled a statue, still and chiseled. After three dates, Avi proposed and she accepted. She waited for him to finish college; she hadn't gone herself. Instead she had taken jobs—more than one, always, because she had too much energy, her mother said. During the day she worked as a receptionist in a dentist's office; some evenings and weekends she worked the Guerlain counter at Bloomingdale's. When Avi took her out—to dances at the JCC or to Asbury Park—he brought her home before twelve. She went to bed wide-eyed and impatient, grateful to have someplace to go the next morning.

In the car on the way into the city, Avi cranked up the heat so her feet wouldn't get cold. The thick glossy cover of a bridal magazine rattled in the breeze from the vent. She turned sideways to face him. At first, she had been intimidated by Avi's lack of expression. Over time she grew to appreciate this steadiness of his; she took it as a sign of his seriousness. The world was full of clowns. She didn't want to marry one.

"Avi, don't you think you'd better tell me what kind of wedding you want?"

Avi's face didn't change. "I don't want a wedding. I just want to be married."

"But what if you don't like—"

The corner of his mouth flicked upward, ever so slightly, and Elaine's insides fluttered. "Whatever you do," he said, "I'll like."

He had recently returned from another summer in Israel and had started working full-time as a civil engineer. According to Elaine's therapist mother, he was experiencing a difficult transition. Elaine agreed: everything that excited her about their new life together—the wedding, buying a house and making it homey—none of it interested Avi. They were supposed to be married in five months and so far had not made any decisions beyond setting the date.

She tried another tack. "Tomorrow, on our way back, we could look at houses in Teaneck."

He didn't take his eyes off the road. "I think I'll be tired. I have to work Monday."

Elaine shifted so she could look out the passenger window. The leaves had just begun to turn, and the weather could go any way at any time: snow flurries could catch you without a jacket; Indian summer could roast you out of your boots. She considered what her mother had told her about college—that not going would put her at a disadvantage. She simply wouldn't have the intellect to keep a college boy interested. "The truth is," her mother had said, "you have no hobbies except for Avi." She read the *Times;* she could always talk about current events, new films, books. Her high-school friends who had gone to college seemed no more or less interesting than she. Most were planning weddings, if not already married. The jobs they held, Elaine felt, were placeholders, something to do until kids came. They met for lunch in the city and discussed china and floor plans, baby names and reception sites. Behind the lipstick smiles and cashmere sweaters of her friends, Elaine couldn't detect any substance very different from her own.

She was slouching again. Lately she had been catching herself hunched over, her shoulders curving in, pressing the upper half of her torso into her lower half, making it difficult to breathe. Her shallow breathing made her drowsy, so that she often felt the urge to nap. She sighed.

"Tired?" Avi said.

"Sleepy." She stretched. She imagined checking into a hotel with Avi, and this revived her momentarily. She sat up straighter.

"Why don't you quit one of your jobs?"

"I like my jobs. I like the people."

"At the dentist's office? You like the screaming children?"

"At the perfume counter. I like the men who buy perfume for their wives."

Avi gave her a small knowing smile. "I take the hint."

"And I like the women who buy perfume for themselves. They have their own money."

"That's why you work two jobs," Avi teased. "When we get married you have to give all your money to me."

Elaine shrieked. "I think it's the other way around."

"It won't matter—it'll be ours." He glanced at her with one of his serious, unreadable looks and stroked her cheek with the back of his hand. She resisted the urge to pull away.

"You can take a nap at Aunt Carol's before the wedding."

The image of rumpled white hotel sheets that she'd been carrying with her for days dissolved. "We're staying there?"

"You are. I'm staying at Tom's studio in the Village."

Elaine slumped in her seat and stared at the creased magazine cover. "I thought we would stay at a hotel. Together."

Avi shook his head. "We're not married, Laney."

She didn't say anything until they reached Aunt Carol's in Murray Hill.

The ceremony was held in a small art gallery in a brownstone uptown. Elaine never would have imagined such a thing. She squeezed Avi's arm as they stood by their chairs waiting for the bride to make her entrance.

"Let's have our wedding here," she said.

"We can have the reception here," Avi said, "but the ceremony has to be at synagogue."

She surveyed the guests, most of whom appeared to be friends of the bride and groom. The women wore silky dresses in jewel tones, and their manicured toes peeked out from dainty sandals. Without thinking about it, Elaine had put on her usual nude hose. She felt dowdy in her long black skirt and pumps. The older relatives kept to the back of the room, as if they believed it in poor taste to make a show of age. She and Avi had arrived slightly late and had also taken seats at the rear of the small room. Two ushers led a frail, stooped man down the aisle. She asked Avi who he was; he hesitated before answering.

"Great-Uncle Lawrence. He sings at everyone's wedding."

She had doubts about Uncle Lawrence's ability to sing. Even with assistance, he could barely walk. The two groomsmen led him to a chair behind the bride and groom's spot. Elaine felt someone should call an ambulance.

A swell of music announced the bride's entrance. Elaine gasped when Avi's cousin stepped into view. She wore a short satin sheath, her legs bare, her tanned skin glowing against the white fabric. As she walked down the aisle, she made eye contact with certain friends and family members, smiling greetings to them. Her groom waited for her, also smiling and clear-eyed. This was not how Elaine had pictured herself on her wedding day. In her mind, she was all but engulfed by her gown; she could barely make out a trace of her dark hair and pale skin amid the layers of white satin and tulle. Her head seemed bowed under the weight of hat and veil. Some force moved her down the aisle; it wasn't clear in her imagination that she even had legs. She craned her neck and stood on tippy-toes to see the bride's feet, tan and lovely in a pair of delicate high-heeled sandals. Elaine remembered her own legs and felt physical and psychic pain. Who wore No nonsense pantyhose? She did, that's who.

When it came time for Uncle Lawrence's part, he swayed slightly in front of his chair. Once he began to sing, his age fell away; if she closed her eyes, she could easily imagine a man of forty or so, old enough to have experienced love, pain, and disappointment, but still vital and strong. She thought she had never heard such a sad and pure voice. When he finished singing, he shrank into himself again and seemed every bit as frail as he had before. The bride and groom sat holding hands, glowing like royalty.

Afterwards, she and Avi followed the crowd to the reception in the building's courtyard. They passed smooth, dark sculptures, the forms of which Elaine couldn't identify: a curve here, a spear or pointed tail there—objects impossible to identify, but something about them stirred her. Gas torches were arranged throughout the courtyard, and Elaine and Avi wove through pockets of heat. Elaine held onto Avi's arm and squeezed.

"Why does Uncle Lawrence sound so sad?" she asked. She expected something romantic—a lost love, an unfulfilled passion, a tragic accident.

Avi stared straight ahead. "He ruined his life."

She knew Avi could be hard on people. "What happened?"

"There's not much to tell. He liked to gamble. His kids won't speak to him. His wife—my mother's aunt—is dead. She was living with us while he hid from the people he owed. Pretty pathetic."

Avi's mother was talking to Uncle Lawrence now, leaning down to him in his chair, smiling, both of them laughing. He could still laugh. She thought about Uncle Lawrence learning of his wife's death, and her throat tightened. "He'll sing at our wedding. To remind us how lucky we are."

"Luck has nothing to do with it," Avi said.

Elaine wiped her eyes. "Blessed, then."

"We choose how we live," Avi said as he steered her toward their table. "It has nothing to do with luck or blessings." He pulled out her chair. "Uncle Lawrence earned his sorrow."

She sat, stunned by his vehemence. "Does every sad person deserve his sorrow?"

"I don't know, Elaine—probably."

She tried to joke. "I'd forgive you, if you lost all our money."

Avi sat beside her, leaned his forearms on the table. "That won't happen."

She knew he was right—nothing like that would ever happen to Avi. He would always be careful never to have regrets. "Mr. Perfect," she said, meaning to joke, but the last syllable caught.

He looked vaguely embarrassed, possibly apologetic. "I'm an engineer. I'm obligated to be correct."

"All the time—your whole life?"

He blushed and looked down at the table. "I'm boring, Elaine, what can I say?"

Avi, she knew, would take pains never to hurt her. She slid her hand over his with genuine affection. "Boring? No." The guests at the next table raised their glasses, and Elaine noted their gleaming elegance. She had never felt as young as they looked. She thought the sooner she and Avi were settled, the better.

She excused herself to the bathroom. In the stall, she peeled off her hose and stuffed them in the trash. "Better," she sighed. The elastic had left a deep red line around her waist, and she vowed never to wear pantyhose again. On the way back to the table, she took longer strides. The satin lining of her skirt thrilled her skin.

She hoped to get Avi on the dance floor; he was a natural, and he'd been taught, though she couldn't say how much he enjoyed it. Usually he humored her with a waltz or a foxtrot.

He was talking to a couple across the table about IRAs. She waited for a pause in the conversation, when she could insert a joke about the dullness of the topic. She tried to catch the eye of the woman, to exchange an exasperated glance, but she appeared just as engrossed as the men. As guests, Elaine thought they were obligated to have fun at the wedding. She thought it bad luck for the newlyweds if the guests were disagreeable or dry. Of course, Avi didn't believe in luck. She sipped her champagne, and when she finished hers, she drank his.

Avi's friend Tom sat next to her. It occurred to her that she might talk to him. He was interning as a reporter at a paper in Florida—she couldn't remember which. They all had internships, she realized, like grownups in training. Tom watched the band and fiddled with a crumpled straw wrapper.

"It must be very interesting, what you do."

Tom regarded her frankly, as if surprised to hear her speak. "You'd think so," he said, looking away again. "Turns out I'm a vulture."

Elaine wasn't sure how to respond, and she was beginning to regret her decision to speak to him.

Tom took another sip of his drink. "What do you ask a man whose son was just devoured by a wood chipper, or the woman whose daughter was found naked in a dumpster?"

"I never thought about it that way," she said.

He gave a wry smile. "Neither had I."

"Well," she said, "someone's got to report on those things, right?"

"Maybe," he said.

She looked down at her hands. "I don't actually read those stories. I don't want to read them."

"Thank you," he said. "I feel so much better now."

She spoke quickly. "It's just an internship. You could do anything you wanted, I'm sure."

"I'll find out, I guess," he said.

"Your job is the opposite of mine. At the perfume counter, people just tell me things."

Tom gave her another mild look of surprise. "Like what?"

"For instance, this woman the other day, buying perfume. She was going to pretend a coworker had given it to her."

"To make her husband jealous?"

"Exactly. Also there's this man who, when he buys perfume for his wife, buys the same for his girlfriend. So he smells the same no matter who he's with."

He smiled. "He told you this?"

"No, I guessed." She finished Avi's champagne. "Don't you just know things sometimes?"

Tom sat back in his chair. "What do you know about me?"

She crossed her legs and leaned closer, as if to tell a secret. "You're different from them," she said, gesturing to their tablemates.

"That's true. I'm not Jewish."

"Not like that." She was a little embarrassed now, and she didn't know how he would respond to what she had to say.

"If you don't tell me, I'll tell Avi you're a shameless flirt."

"He won't believe you." In fact, she had no idea what Avi thought about her. How would he describe her? Serious? Pretty? Smart enough? She felt suddenly defensive and delivered her judgment of Tom more passionately than she'd intended. "I bet that none of the people at this table would admit they'd made a mistake about their careers. That's how you're different. You have guts."

Tom smiled a little and rattled the ice in his glass. "We'll see. Drink?"

She didn't bother alerting Avi, who was now engaged with the couple beside him. Tom placed his hand at the small of her back and guided her to the bar. Avi never touched her this way, and she found this careless gesture of Tom's more exciting than Avi's goodnight kisses. At the bar, Tom surveyed the crowd while they waited. "So, what do you think of the happy couple? Think they'll make it?"

"No wonder people don't want to talk to you. You're awfully blunt."

Tom laughed. "You like the direct approach, I can tell."

This was the first time she thought he might be drunk. She stared at the newlyweds: the bride in her cocktail dress, the groom in his Brooks Brothers suit. She guessed they would honeymoon in Jamaica and live on Long Island.

"They seem right for each other."

He nodded. "Tactful. Very tactful."

"What about you? Will they live happily ever after?"

"Yes. But she'll have an affair."

She slapped his arm. "That's not very nice."

"It'll be a wake-up call for him. He'll ignore her and get too involved in his work. She'll feel lonely and neglected."

Their drinks came. Tom placed his hand on her back, and she shivered. "She'll have an affair and get caught—on purpose."

"He'll divorce her," she said, watching Avi, who leaned back in his chair and appeared to sigh. She wondered what he was so impatient to do.

"He'll beg forgiveness and commit himself to a period of unseemly devotion."

"What!" She dragged her gaze back to Tom. "Why?"

He slid his hand to her shoulder and squeezed. "You are so lovely and naïve," he murmured. "Avi's a lucky bastard."

Elaine blushed.

"C'mon," he said. "Let's dance."

The reception ended too soon. Elaine and Tom were left panting and sweating in the middle of the courtyard. The last song had been "Shout," and Tom had gotten down on his back and Elaine had stood over him, resting her foot on his chest as if to hold him there. When he rose, the gray silhouette of her shoe showed on his white shirt-front. He said exactly what she was thinking.

"We're not finished dancing." He swept her back to the table, where Avi was shrugging into his jacket. He gave every appearance of wanting to call it a night.

"Have fun?" he asked Elaine.

"Lots. I missed you on the dance floor."

"No, she didn't," Tom said to Avi. He turned to Elaine, and she marveled at how green his eyes were, now that their rims were so red. "You shouldn't lie to him."

Avi smiled a little, but Elaine blushed.

Tom talked Avi into going to a jazz club in the Village. Elaine clomped along in her heels, hanging on Tom's big arm. He was meatier than Avi, and seemed made for holding onto. Avi was more like smoke, Elaine thought. You could sense his presence, but you could never be sure just how much of him was really there. He walked slightly apart from them, his hands in his pockets. He answered questions when asked, and talked to Tom, but Elaine found him curiously unresponsive to her. Tom, on the other hand, encouraged her every conversational whim. They talked easily about nothing much. During the first lull in conversation, Tom put his arm around Elaine and drew her close to his side.

"Avi, I have a confession to make."

Elaine shivered, the coolness of the night finally penetrating.

Avi turned toward them. She wondered what he thought of Tom's handling of her. She wished some of his manner would rub off on Avi. "Oh?" Avi said. "What's that?"

"It's a two-part confession." He looked at Elaine and pulled her closer with every word, so that her feet barely skimmed the sidewalk. "One, I adore your bride."

Avi murmured, "Oh, you do, do you?" She thought he sounded

slightly sinister, and she understood Tom's compliment was for Avi, not for her.

"Two: your bride has inspired me to make good on my threat to join the Peace Corps. I'm going to Africa."

Avi's amusement evaporated, and he gave Tom a look—stern and disapproving—that she recognized and dreaded. Despite his disapproval, she couldn't help exclaiming over the news. "What will you do there?"

"Teach, observe, write. After two years, I should have enough material for a book. If I don't, well, I could have done worse things with my life."

Avi shook his head. "Better to get it out of your system now, before you start a family."

Tom laughed. Elaine said, "You talk like it's a disease. It sounds exciting."

"Romantic notions are a disease," Avi said.

Elaine looked at Tom pleadingly.

"Don't you know who you're marrying?" Tom said. "This is classic Avi." It seemed funny to her in the moment, and she and Tom laughed.

At the entrance to the club, Avi held the door open for them. The place was full and Elaine had to squeeze between two tables to take her seat on the banquette. An older man sat very near to her. Tom had to pull the table out so he could squeeze beside her.

"I hope you don't mind, Avi, but you'll have her the rest of your life, right?"

"Right," Avi said.

Two bourbon-and-Cokes arrived for Elaine, who was already drunk. "What's this?"

"It's called a double," Tom said. "Cheers."

Avi watched the band. Elaine drank her first cocktail quickly, to get rid of it. She was sipping her second when she started to feel unwell. As she made her way to the bathroom, the floor buckled in jagged hunks, rising and falling beneath her feet. The bathroom wobbled and heaved. She stood at the sink gripping its cool sides, hoping to vomit. Her eyes watered, and her belches echoed off the tiles. Feeling no better, she lurched back to the table, keeping her eyes on the violently shifting floor. Tom wouldn't let her sit. He tried to dance with her, but she bounced off his chest like a doll. By the time he led her back to their seats, most of her vision had blackened, save for small portholes of wavering amber. When she squeezed between the two tables, her legs became liquid rushing to the floor, and she collapsed into the lap of the elderly man next to them, bracing herself on his crotch. Startled, he jumped, and Elaine slid between his legs to the floor beneath the table.

For a moment, she rested her cheek against the cool pedestal of the table. If she could just rest and breathe some cool air. Tom flipped the tablecloth up and beckoned. "Come. This way." She crawled out, and once Tom had lifted her to her feet, she marched stiff-legged to the door. Avi was already hailing a cab. She had hit her head and scraped her arm, and now she clutched herself in a shamed embrace on the sidewalk. "Ow, ow, ow," she said.

Tom came out with their coats over his arm. "Are you all right, sweetheart?"

"I scraped my arm. I feel sick."

She threw up twice out the window of the cab on the way to Aunt Carol's. Tom spoke loudly and continuously to the driver, to cover the sound of her retching. When they arrived at the brownstone, Avi held her elbow and led her upstairs. Sick and humiliated, she pulled away and wobbled ahead of him. In the bedroom, half-undressed, she turned to look at her arm where Avi had held her. No trace of him.

She awoke in the morning with what felt like a mortal head wound. She heard, as if from a great depth, Aunt Carol say, "She's still sleeping." Later, she woke to pounding on the door. The pounding wouldn't stop. Aunt Carol, apparently, was out. Elaine wove through the rooms toward the sound, bumping into doorframes and occasional tables, upsetting photographs and rattling candy dishes. She answered the door wearing only her slip. It was Tom, and he held her purse.

"You left it at the club. I'm not sure if anything's missing. I didn't want to look."

Heat rose to her cheeks. She took her purse and waved him in. He stepped into the small warm kitchen, his hands shoved into his pockets. She smelled alcohol and hoped the smell wasn't coming from her.

"Avi noticed, so we went back. The old guy you fell on must have turned it in to the bartender."

Elaine looked inside. Everything was there, but her wallet had been emptied of cash.

"Where's Avi?" She imagined him waiting in the car outside. Would he be blank-faced or disapproving? Her mouth felt suddenly juicy.

Tom looked pained. "He went back to Jersey. He asked me to put you on a train. He said to call when you get to the station."

Now her eyes stung, and she looked down into her purse again. Tom would have to give her money for the train and for the phone, too. Why couldn't Avi have waited—or at least left her money for the train? She clicked her purse shut. "I'm not going."

Tom nodded, as if that were the only thing to do—the thing he could have predicted and in fact wanted her to do. He waited while she showered and dressed, brought her a glass of ginger ale after a fit of vomiting. When they said good-bye, he kissed her cheek. "Good luck in Africa," she said, "and with your book." Her engagement to Avi already felt like a mostly forgotten dream.

With the money she had been saving for the wedding, she sublet a friend's studio in the Village, on West 11th. At first her mother was pleased about her change of plans. She thought Avi too old-fashioned, too conservative, too Jewish. When she finally understood Elaine's plans—that they didn't include college—she became disturbed once again. Elaine found it easy to ignore her mother's misgivings.

II

Nine years after she had moved to the Village, she was robbed on a Saturday in early June. That morning she sipped coffee on the balcony, easing into the day. Her legs were bare, and she wore nothing but a large white button-down and panties. A beer truck pulled up to the liquor store across the street, and a man unloaded cases onto a hand truck. This was her Saturday routine: a date with the beer man. She liked to air-dry her hair, it was too hot for much clothing, and the skirts girls wore were shorter than her shirt. The beer man didn't seem to mind.

She'd been blond now for five years. She'd grown her hair out and bleached it, her eyebrows too. Sometimes she tanned.

"Blondie," the man called. "You got a sandwich for me?"

"I'll give you a sandwich."

"I'll get in trouble with my wife."

"Just for a sandwich?"

"See you next week." He got in his truck and drove away.

After putting on a pair of jeans, she got her basket and detergent and set out for the laundry room. She thought about keys, but her jeans were too tight and she was afraid she'd lose them, so she left the door unlocked. When she came back to her apartment, she sat at the table and called her mother. Mrs. Shapiro was dating someone new, and Elaine enjoyed calling weekend mornings to talk to Ernie while he made breakfast for her mother.

"Ma, put Ernie on."

Her mother sighed. "Ernie, it's your girlfriend."

Ernie said, "Alice, I tell her it's over. She keeps calling. I don't know why."

"Listen, Ernie, I need a favor," Elaine said.

Ernie wheezed into the phone. "Anything, doll."

Elaine liked asking her mother's boyfriends for favors. She had never been resentful of her mother's dating; in fact, she had always considered her mother's beaux potential resources for all sorts of things. The trick was figuring out what they were good for. Most were grateful for the interest, and, Elaine discovered, they liked helping and being appreciated. She never thought much about what she brought to the table, other than gratitude. She hit Ernie up for a workshop on networking for the young professionals of the JCC. He was flattered and agreed.

Her mother got on the phone. Elaine worried vaguely about her laundry. A peach silk camisole had disappeared recently when she'd forgotten her clothes overnight. "Hi, Mommy. What's up?"

"Are you nervous about your big night?"

Elaine answered firmly. "It'll run itself. And Daniel will be there for moral support."

She could almost hear her mother's tight-lipped frown. "There's someone I want you to meet—a dermatologist, just your age and so handsome! He knows about art, too—he's not just some, you know, stethoscope."

Elaine closed her eyes. "Daniel will be there, Mom."

"What—you can't meet someone? Is Daniel that insecure? Sometimes young men are, you know."

The eggs and butter in her mother's kitchen sizzled over the line.

"Mommy, I love you, but I have to check my laundry."

She raced down to the basement to move her clothes to the dryer, again leaving the door unlocked. When she returned she called Daniel, who worked at the JCC with her. They talked for sixty minutes, flirting and making plans to meet that night before the fundraiser. Daniel had been waging an elaborate campaign to persuade Elaine to spend six months in the Catskills at his uncle's cabin. He had received a grant to pursue a new photography project.

"Remind me," Elaine said, "what I would be doing at your uncle's cabin for six months."

On the other end of the line, Daniel inhaled sharply. There was a long pause before he spoke. "Nature," he said. "You'd be part of nature." He exhaled.

"We went camping once, with some neighbors. Nightmare! Burrs in my socks, ticks in every crevice."

Daniel moaned drowsily. "I will personally—" He inhaled again.

"Yes?"

"—attend to—"

"Uh-huh—"

"—every inch," he exhaled, "of Elaine Shapiro. No terrain unexplored. Meticulous mapping. Don't. You. Worry."

Elaine giggled madly. "I'll visit weekends. You'll have to do all the mapmaking then."

"You'll try to leave," Daniel said, "but you will stay, stay, stay."

After their good-byes, feeling sultry, Elaine rescued her overheated laundry from the dryer.

That evening, she shimmied into a bronze satin slip dress and matching sandals. She opened her vanity to find her pearl earrings missing. The gold bracelet Avi had given her long ago was also gone. After rummaging through all the drawers, she straightened up and looked around the room. The little box of change and stamps on the shelf had been opened—the lid was off, the change gone. The box of photographs and old cards that she kept on the coffee table had also been opened. Nothing seemed missing aside from the change and her jewelry. She realized someone must have come into the apartment while she had been in the basement. The lobby door could only be opened with a key, and she wondered which of her neighbors could have trespassed. She imagined Mrs. Otseke in her flowery kimono opening the fridge to examine the leftovers, Mr. Safransky mashing the white bathmat in his street shoes. Maybe the guest of another tenant had robbed her—the stringy-haired saxophone player hosted a stream of gigging musicians, and the librarian was putting up his teenaged sister whom Elaine thought of as "Cornfield," because she was from Ohio, even though she had been introduced to the girl at least twice. She imagined the raven-haired girl, watchful, waiting for her moment, slipping in and rustling through Elaine's things. Elaine stepped into the hallway and peered down both ends, gazing at each green door as if she could note a sign of guilt or spy her missing items with the X-ray vision of the righteous. She didn't bother calling the police.

Daniel arrived, as always, with a camera.

"This is a Brownie," he told Elaine, holding up the small box. He snapped her picture after she'd turned away from locking the door—which she made a show of doing, noisily rattling her keys and throwing all the bolts. She felt stupid about the loss of her jewelry—it was her fault for leaving the door unlocked—and she didn't feel like mentioning it. She was afraid she might cry if he showed sympathy, and she felt bereft enough as it was. She wore her everyday earrings—gold filigree studs her mother had given her for her sixteenth birthday.

"You have enough pictures of me. Let me take yours."

Daniel handed over the odd box of a camera.

"Turn sideways."

She looked through the viewfinder and marveled at his unlined skin, his fine nose and hazel eyes. She, Elaine Shapiro, was dating a god—a god who lusted for her. She snapped the picture. They kissed long and hard, Elaine pressing Daniel into Mrs. Otseke's door.

On the way to the train, she held onto Daniel's forearm, kneading it. "Tell me more about the Catskills," she said, tossing her hair.

Daniel glanced at her. "Wait—you're actually considering?"

"Were you not serious about the invitation?"

He stopped in front of her, held both of her hands. "I'm completely serious. Take a leave of absence—that's what I'm doing." He paused. "This could be a trial run for us."

Elaine's heart lurched, and she felt her eyes widen. "Or not," Daniel said.

"Ha," she said. "You can't have it both ways."

They started walking again. "Why can it only be two ways?" he said.

"Because," Elaine said, "I only went to high school. They only teach two ways."

"My God, my parents would probably pay you to go back to school, they love you so much."

"They love the idea of me," Elaine said. "Your father does, anyway. Well, maybe your mother."

She thought of playing cards with Daniel's mother, how they'd gotten drunk and Mrs. Eisenman had shown her the gowns she'd worn to yesterday's formals, insisting that Elaine model them. She had beamed—warm nostalgia!—and Elaine had cooked up a fundraiser on the spot: for the ladies of the JCC to pay to see their idealized pasts floating down the runway toward them. Now she entertained the possibility once again of being taken care of; she liked the idea of being rich in resources—Mr. and Mrs. Eisenman, Daniel's uncle, people who enjoyed the idea of a young couple's potential. She imagined waking up to Daniel gathering his cameras and preparing for the day. She could keep working part-time, cook meals for them, make a home, find clever ways to throw dinner parties on a budget, something she was already good at, on a much larger scale—with other people's money. They would have whimsical low-budget vacations in the off-season, at other people's cottages. Or maybe she would become someone entirely new, a person she could not now imagine. College. The Catskills, spring and summer. Why say no?

She matched Daniel's long stride, her heart pounding. "What do you see in the forest?"

"Trees, mostly," he said. He stopped again and faced her. "You can do whatever you want. Come and go as you please. OK?"

She nodded and they walked again, Elaine pressing to keep up with him. She was beginning to feel harried by the pace, so she tried to focus on the people passing by, tried to see inside them for some clue: Whimsical or serious? Depressed or fulfilled? Grateful or bitter? Steadfast or uncertain? Finally, she stopped in the middle of the sidewalk. "You're running me off my feet here."

Daniel whirled around to retrieve her. "Hiking boots," he said.

A woman passing by smiled at them. Elaine wondered what she saw.

At the dinner dance, Daniel moved among the crowd snapping pictures for future brochures and fundraising campaigns. Elaine liked this arrangement; she could mingle without having to worry about entertaining him, but he was there and he was hers. As she talked to the partygoers, she found herself distracted by the women's jewelry. She felt a pang every time she saw a pair of earrings like her stolen pair, or even unlike them. The bracelet she had felt guilty about keeping, but her mother had assured her that returning it to Avi would seem strange and spiteful. If this were some kind of karmic payback, well then, time to move on, but every woman outfitted in pearls or diamonds or weighted down with gold had a man nearby, and each one held onto the arm of her man like an anchor. Elaine, in her slip of a dress and her minuscule earrings, felt in danger of floating away.

She shook away the feeling and turned to find Daniel. She scanned the room and saw again the many women in dark gowns glimmering in the low light. Faint panic fluttered against her ribs as she slowly turned. Scanning the room again she saw him behind the serving table, squatting amid the black-clad legs of the caterers, photographing the milk crates filled with dirty plates, cups, and utensils.

At this moment, her mother swept into the room, leading a tuxedo-clad Ernie by the hand. At fifty-five, Mrs. Shapiro had what Elaine liked to consider substance. It wasn't entirely looks; it had something to do with her mother's presence and the way she carried herself. Elaine could never pull off the things her mother wore. The cappuccino-colored gown this evening, for instance, with the matching stole. On her mother the gown was regal; Elaine would have looked like a girl playing dress-up. Mrs. Shapiro spotted her and glided over with Ernie. They kissed each other in greeting, and her mother frowned.

"You look flushed. What's wrong?"

Ernie went to get drinks, and Mrs. Shapiro dabbed at Elaine's forehead with a tissue. Maybe her mother would decide not to introduce her to the doctor if she were sweating too much. She considered telling her mother about the robbery, in fact, wanted to, but she knew her mother would worry about her safety and might even insist that Elaine come live with her in Chatham. Elaine feared she might agree.

"I'm fine." She took her mother's hand and squeezed. "Now, where's this art-loving doctor?"

Mrs. Shapiro led Elaine across the dance floor to meet Paul, the dermatologist. Ernie sailed toward them with their drinks on a tray commandeered from one of the staff. After the introductions and preliminary chitchat, he and Mrs. Shapiro excused themselves. Elaine liked Paul's dark looks and his cool light fingers in her hand when they were introduced. They talked about their jobs, and while they talked, Elaine imagined his enormous loft apartment, how dim and expensive it would be. She saw herself sitting on a butter-soft leather sofa, tastefully dressed and flipping through a magazine. She wanted to say, "I'm sure you're very nice," but she didn't know how to finish the thought.

"You're really very lovely," he said. Elaine gave him a sharp look. She agreed to meet him for drinks the following Tuesday. On the one hand, what was the harm? On the other, what was the point? After they parted company, she eyed the people around her. As she had predicted, the party ran itself. People showed up, the caterers served food, and the guests ate, drank, talked, and laughed. Daniel had switched cameras and used the telephoto lens to snap pictures of the guests. His blue sharkskin suit glimmered. Two women in black cocktail dresses watched him from the edge of the room. The women exchanged glances, then burst out laughing. Elaine wanted to throw her soda water in their faces, though she knew that their laughter could have been innocent. She made her rounds, checking that the food stations were stocked and the tables reasonably cleared. Along the way, she chatted with guests and discussed plans for renovation of the community center and the new art classes being offered in the fall.

Paul interrupted her rounds and asked her to dance. "Nice party," he said. "I'm impressed."

Elaine shrugged off the compliment, though she was pleased. "Once you've thrown one party for two hundred, you've done it."

"But you're so young."

Elaine laughed. "We're the same age. What did my mother tell you?"

"She was completely discreet," he said. "She's very proud of you."

"That's generous of you," Elaine said. "And I'm really sorry."

"I'm not," he said.

She preferred to let a good dancer lead, and Paul could dance—nothing flashy, but he knew what he was doing, and he wasn't timid about holding her. When she complimented him, he insisted that she was the good dancer.

"I don't want to fight about it," she said. He pulled her closer.

The same two women who had been watching Daniel now watched her. Elaine squinted at them. When the song finished and Paul escorted her off the floor, she made a point of talking to them.

"I hope you're enjoying the party."

The tall one regarded her frankly. "Not as much as you are, kid. Two men. I should be so lucky."

The plump one arched her brow. "Who wants trouble? I can't keep up." The women scanned the crowd behind her. Elaine knew these women were her age—it was true they both had families and households to run, as she had once planned, if not with Avi then around him. Somehow they thought themselves much older. She thought this a fault of theirs and not a result necessarily of being married and having children. Look at her mother, after all: wasn't she still vital and gorgeous?

She took up the hand of the tall woman, whose features were very sharp. "Let me read your palm. I'm practicing for the next fundraiser—it's a carnival." The woman's hand felt heavy with rings and bracelets. She tapped the woman's palm. "Here—the love line. You're going to meet someone who will change your life forever."

The woman turned to her companion. "She must be talking about Mike's mistress." The two of them laughed so sharply that Elaine flinched. They picked their way through the crowd, settling in another corner from which they could survey the scene without being disturbed. Elaine continued to circulate, and the women's laughter seemed to follow her. She became more and more animated; told louder, funnier stories; flirted with everyone, male and female. She plastered a smile on her face, helped people with their coats, and made appointments for coffee, lunch, planning.

After the last patrons had slipped into cabs, Mrs. Shapiro invited Elaine and Daniel out for breakfast before heading home. Elaine and her mother walked arm in arm while Daniel walked backwards in front of them, taking pictures. Ernie had gone ahead for the car. Elaine's feet felt bruised, and her face ached from smiling. "It's late, Mommy. Don't you need to get home to the suburbs?"

"I like to spend time with you kids. You make me feel young."

"I feel like Methuselah."

"Which is why," Daniel said, "you need to come to the Catskills with me. Tell her, Alice."

To Daniel, Mrs. Shapiro said, "I believe in the restorative powers of a change of scenery."

Daniel smiled at Elaine as if to say, See?

At Lox Around the Clock, all the things Daniel did when they were alone together made her wince in public. The way he sang to himself, the way he couldn't stop fiddling with his cameras: Elaine said silent prayers that he would be still for just a moment. Ernie was visibly distressed. He looked around the diner, trying to focus his attention away from the table, while Mrs. Shapiro kept up a veiled conversation about Paul the dermatologist.

"Paul was telling me about real estate in Montana. Wonderful place for a second home."

"Are you thinking of buying there?" Elaine asked.

Mrs. Shapiro shrugged elaborately. "Who knows? We could end up anywhere. We all could." She settled her gaze on Daniel, who was tying a straw wrapper in a knot.

"Alice," Daniel said, "maybe you could provide some insight."

Elaine turned to face Daniel. His eyes were red-rimmed. When had he? In the bathroom at the party probably, and her annoyance, an ever-renewable source, flared.

Mrs. Shapiro folded her hands in front of her on the table. "I'm always happy to help."

Elaine could have supplied her mother's thoughts: I'm always happy to help an inappropriate young man pack his bags. She leaned back against the booth to watch the scene play out.

"How can I get your daughter to come away with me to the Catskills?"

Mrs. Shapiro turned her gaze to Elaine, who thought her mother was doing a passable job of suppressing a great deal of mirthful malevolence. "Well," she said. "What would she do for six months in the country?"

"That's exactly what she said." Daniel nudged Elaine. "Like mother like daughter. I'm beginning to think I should disinvite you. No offense," he said to Alice.

Elaine's mother continued to smile serenely at Daniel. "We're long past the days of girls following boys wherever they may go," she said.

"Women," Daniel said. "We call them women now."

"See!" Mrs. Shapiro exclaimed.

By the time the food came, Elaine was exhausted and cranky. Beside her, Daniel jiggled his leg in time to the 1950s rock and roll on the jukebox. She placed her hand on his upper thigh and stroked, lazily, lightly, as if a pleasant afterthought; this kept him still for the rest of the meal, and they ate in relative peace.

He hung on her all the way from Lincoln Center. They stood in the middle of the subway car, Elaine holding onto a pole, Daniel holding on to Elaine. He ran his hands all over her, sliding the satiny fabric of her dress as he fondled her belly and the underside of her breasts. Every once in a while he'd press into her and she'd feel him against her, hard.

Back at her apartment, he sat naked on the ottoman; Elaine, who had forgotten his annoying habits, straddled him. He held her tight against his hairless body, so tight that she could barely move. At first this excited her. After a time she found she couldn't inhale any air that hadn't just been exhaled by Daniel. The more she tried to pull away or change position, the more closely he held her. Finally, she couldn't take a breath, or at least she thought she couldn't; later he told her that was impossible—he couldn't have been holding her that tight. But she had passed out—right in the middle of things.

III

At forty-two, she still felt like a girl. When she walked home from the subway, she felt the energy of the city. It shot up her legs, suffusing her muscles, sending tingling waves through her torso. The energy of the city crackled through her and out of her—through her smile, through the spark in her eyes.

She had settled into a routine: weekdays fundraising for WNYC and weekends at Hudson Flowers at the corner of Hudson and W. 11th. She had been dating comfortably, for three years, a married man named Joe, with whom she worked at WNYC. She had moved into a larger apartment on Thompson Street. Her balcony, on the third floor, faced a jazz club, and sometimes at night she stood outside in her silk robe with a glass of white wine and watched the musicians load in. Weekends, she often had brunch at the Hudson Café, across the street from the flower shop.

This morning, she could not get past the picture of the Kennedy wedding in the *Times*. It was the ten-year anniversary of the plane crash, so all the papers were running the same picture: the couple framed by the doorway of the small church on Cumberland Island where they had married. She sat at the café sipping coffee before opening the shop. Rain dripped from the vinyl awning and blew underneath, spattering the paper. She drummed her fingers on the table. They were so young and so impossibly well-groomed. What had her mother said? "A well-bred couple." She shifted her gaze to the cuffs of her black jeans, which were starting to fray. Then she looked at the picture again. "Such fluid grace! Such simplicity!" Her mother had practically broken into song. Elaine rolled her eyes and folded the paper. She and Joe would go out tonight—an oddity. Normally she had him during the week and his family got him on the weekends. This was a special exception—their three-year anniversary. She had splurged and bought a new dress—a new old dress at a vintage shop in the Village. It was sleek and black and reminded her of Audrey Hepburn in *Breakfast at Tiffany's*.

She paid her check and made her way across the street. One of the owners might stop by for a few hours on either day, but for the rest of the time she worked alone. She enjoyed the quiet closeness of the shop. It was small and subterranean, with steps leading down to the entrance. She unlocked the iron gate and then the door. During nicer weather, she set buckets of gladioli and spider mums out on the walk. Mostly she stayed indoors and drank coffee, opened her mail, caught up on her correspondence and phone calls, and paid bills. Occasionally she made up bouquets and wrapped them in lavender tissue for customers. Joe sometimes came to visit, but not so often since he had moved his family to Summit.

Before she closed up on Saturdays, she made a bouquet for herself, for which she never paid. At first she used the slightly old flowers, the ones no one would buy. After a short while she felt no compunction using the freshest: sweet pea, Oriental lilies, lily of the valley, Johnny jump-ups, Gerbera daisy, bird of paradise. Hal, one of the owners, had taught her how to open the bird of paradise, to slit the green sheath with a knife and pull out the orange and purple petals within. She had thought, like most, that the blossoms would unfurl on their own, in their own time. Actually, they had to be coaxed. If left to their devices, the flowers would burst forth at the last possible moment; they would start to fade immediately. She took great pleasure in these little gifts to herself; she felt herself a rich and extravagant benefactress. She never took carnations. They depressed her. Too common.

This Saturday she was somewhat disturbed, though she was more interested in elevating her mood than in determining what bothered her. The air smelled somewhat fresher than usual. It had a been a moist spring, and now the humidity of summer crept in, weighing down the air, until in late July to go outside would feel like being wrapped from head to foot in a wet wool blanket. For now, though, the air felt light and cool, and she wished she were meeting Joe for champagne brunch at Hudson Café—or anywhere. Yes, why not someplace different? She sighed harshly as she bent to lift a bucket of miniature pink carnations. She felt tired—a little draggy—and her knees ached, though she couldn't say why. She had the usual bills to pay and mail to sort, which she saved all week for this mostly idle time. Today she was particularly grateful for the quiet.

She was facing two neat stacks of bills and catalogs when the bell over the shop door rang. She looked up to see a young couple enter. The woman was blond and athletic-looking—no makeup, but bright skin and light eyes. They held hands as they came down the steps, both of them giggling and flushed as they fit themselves through the narrow passage. The young man smoothed his dark hair from his forehead.

"We need some flowers," he said, "for a wedding."

She smiled at them, though she felt a persistent tug somewhere behind her eyes.

"When's the date?"

The blonde looked up at the young man. "Today," she said. "In a few minutes."

Elaine looked at the young man for confirmation. He raised his eyebrows at her. "We're tying the knot and hitting the trail."

The girl laughed. "Then we'll speak to each other in clichés for the rest of our lives."

Elaine noted that they both wore backpacks—how could she have missed that? She fixed a boutonniere of sweet pea for the groom and a small bouquet of sweet pea and Gerbera daisies for the bride. The girl excused herself to use the bathroom, and Elaine asked the groom about the honeymoon. They were hiking the Appalachian Trail, which would take a good six months, the young man told her. After that, they were moving to Africa. "I never would have thought of such a thing," she admitted. She pinned the boutonniere to the man's backpack strap. "Nice touch," he said. She looked into his face and thought he looked vaguely underdone—a cake pulled from the oven too soon—and she had to laugh at herself.

The girl, meanwhile, seemed to be having difficulties in the bathroom. Elaine thought she might have forgotten to replace the paper, so she went to check. She knocked on the door just as the girl opened it. The girl flashed a big smile.

"Hey," she said. "Had to shoot up for the big day."

Elaine gave her a quizzical look.

"I'm diabetic," the girl said.

Elaine imagined the trail littered with hypodermics. She thought it must be juvenile diabetes, and she wondered how it would affect the girl's life; she'd heard that they couldn't have children. She had never seen a person look so young and healthy. She watched as they fit themselves through the narrow stairwell to the door, their packs bumping against each other.

That night, dinner took close to three hours: raw oysters, champagne, spring pea soup, Beef Wellington, fruit, cheese, more champagne, and chocolate soufflé. They went dancing afterwards, though both of them were so full and drowsy they didn't last long. Elaine shivered in her sleeveless gown, and Joe draped his jacket over her shoulders. She tilted her head so she could smell his cologne. Elaine loved Joe's clothes. They smelled expensive. She clasped his hand as they walked and rested her head for a moment on his big arm. When she straightened herself up again, he was looking at her strangely, she thought, as if he'd realized she was much drunker than he was.

They took a carriage to the Plaza. Elaine wanted to order room service. She wanted to use the giant tub and rub her face in all the towels.

"Tomorrow," Joe said.

"You have to go home tomorrow," she said.

So they ordered more champagne. They crammed themselves into the tub, which wasn't as big as it had appeared. While lolling there, Elaine started to speak several times but stopped. Joe didn't speak either. Normally they chatted about people at work, or Elaine reported details from the fundraising parties she'd been to. Generally they laughed and made fun. Tonight, though, Elaine felt they should talk of weightier matters, it being their anniversary. She felt dull and heavy from the food. She set her glass down on the tile floor. "I'm going to get my hair wet." She slid down until her head was covered. Joe shifted while she was underwater, and for a panicky second she thought he might try to hold her there. But then he shifted again, and she realized he was probably uncomfortable. She raised herself up and smoothed her wet hair away from her face. Joe was getting out of the tub.

"Where are you going?"

"Out. I'm pruning." He wrapped a thick white towel around his waist.

The water felt suddenly too warm. Elaine leaned back against the cool porcelain. Joe sat on the edge of the tub, and she noted for the first time the few white hairs that had crept into his mustache. "Well," he said. "Enjoying your anniversary?"

She smiled at him and nodded. "You?"

He palmed her cheek. "Come out of the water. You're falling asleep."

When she came out of the bathroom, the room was dark. She tiptoed around the bed, felt for her side as her eyes adjusted. "Joe?" His breathing was slow. She could just make out the lump of him. Naked, she sat on the edge of the bed. The sheets felt cool. She slid under the covers and laid her head down, then jerked upright. Something cold and hard was on her pillow. She turned on the bedside lamp and found a necklace of ivory-colored pearls with a diamond clasp. She put it around her neck—a choker—and curled into Joe's warm body.

The next morning they awoke hungover, tired, and cranky. Elaine wore her new necklace with a wrap dress she had bought at a consignment shop. She appraised her reflection in the mirror, touched her fingers to the pearls. Before she could stop herself, she squinted. The pearls felt heavy against her collarbone. Behind her, Joe pushed his hairy belly against her back. "Move it, lady. It's my turn in here."

She thought of the young couple hiking the Appalachian Trail. They probably wore only simple wedding bands as they slipped through the woods. She turned away from the mirror, patting Joe's hairy gut.

"You're very hairy, and I'm afraid I have to leave you."

"Don't let the door hit you—"

"We're not married. You can't speak to me in clichés." She peered over her shoulder at herself in the mirror. "Is it appropriate to wear a pearl choker during the daytime?"

"Pearls are for anytime, pearls are for always. You go to the bathroom in them. You get married in them. You visit your coke dealer in them."

"But a choker? I know preps wear pearls 24/7, but a choker is so . . ."

"Slutty?"

"That's not the word I was looking for. When you wear a choker, it's like you have something to prove."

Joe combed his hair in the mirror. "Are you trying to tell me you don't want the necklace? Don't wear it if you don't want it, but I won't take it back."

Elaine folded her arms over her chest. "Maybe I'd prefer something else."

Joe combed his mustache. He replied without moving his upper lip. "Prefer all you want."

Elaine laughed loudly. "You are such an asshole."

"You've been talking to Marianne."

She hugged him and pressed her cheek into his furry shoulder. "I don't need to compare notes with your wife. You were a lousy date last night."

He stopped combing. "I know."

She patted his shoulder and gave him a soft kiss on the lips. "Bye-bye," she said.

In the elevator, she caught sight of her reflection in the polished metal of the closed doors. The plunging neckline of the dark purple sundress contrasted nicely with her pale skin. The India-print fabric was so light she imagined that if a breeze caught it, the dress would unwrap itself and be carried off by the wind. She had bobbed her hair and dyed it a deep auburn. She lifted her chin at her reflection. Not bad, she thought. Something about the necklace still irked her, the way it made itself known—felt—the clammy weight of it at the base of her throat. She slipped her finger beneath the strand, as if to stretch it out. She undid the clasp and held the necklace loosely in her fist. She had told her mother she would come by for brunch with Ernie, who was recently home after his bypass. As she walked to the subway, she imagined letting the heavy strand slip through her fingers. What would she do with such a thing? And why had Joe given it to her? It was hard for her to imagine the wardrobe that would complement this particular piece of jewelry. A fur coat? With nothing but implants and a fake tan beneath. She dropped the necklace into the depths of her oversized bag. Her cell phone rang. It was Joe.

"For God's sake, what?" she said.

"I'm an ass," he said.

"You dialed the phone for that?"

"It was a stupid present. So not you."

"I gave it to a homeless woman."

"Serves me right." He paused, and she waited. "I wanted to show you, to tell you—"

"Show and tell, hm?"

"OK. Enough. We both know it was a mistake."

"These things happen to rich people who are spread too thin," Elaine said.

"Some sympathy, please, for a mortal man."

"That was it," Elaine said. "You missed it."

She was smiling now, poised at the stairs leading down to the subway. "I have to go," she said. "I'm at the train. I'll lose you."

She took the PATH train out of the city and walked the five blocks from the station to the house her mother shared with Ernie. She felt the walk would do her good, work the last of the champagne out of her system and clear her head. The morning felt bright and sharp. She started to call ahead, then hung up. Of course the coffee would be on.

She let herself in through the back door, which opened into a vestibule through which one walked to the kitchen. The room had been a tiny sun porch and was now a laundry room with a view, as her mother described it. Through the French doors to the kitchen, Elaine watched her mother settling Ernie at the table. She heard the tones of their conversation, but not the words. She didn't want to interrupt. Ernie spoke, and he gazed up at his wife from his seat, waiting to be delighted by her reply. Elaine recognized her mother's tone—sassy, jokingly disrespectful. Ernie had willingly provided the setup, so that she could dazzle him with the punch line. He laughed and grabbed her hand, swinging. His tone said, "You are something, kid." Elaine's mother smiled and took Ernie's chin in her hand. They kissed, and she gave his cheek a playful slap. Elaine reached up to her neck to touch the pearls. Then she remembered she'd put them in her bag.

She pushed through the door and cleared her throat elaborately, making a low bow. Ernie and her mother shouted out to her.

"Now we can open the champagne," Ernie said.

Elaine made a sour face. She couldn't stop it coming. "Welcome home," she said. "How was the hospital?"

"Eh," Ernie said, "I'm alive. I can't complain."

"He'll insist that we drink mimosas," her mother said.

Ernie lifted his arms from the table, the maroon bells of his bathrobe sleeves sliding down his arms. Green and yellow bruises marked his skin. "I do insist. Someone's got to have a good time for me."

"I'll do my best," Elaine said, swallowing carefully.

Ernie clasped his hands in front of him on the table and said, "So, kid—tell me, what's new?"

She hadn't told them about Joe and couldn't begin to now. The last three years of assignations she had presented to Ernie and her mother as a series of mostly unrelated vignettes, featuring subjects at times who were mythical or legendary, antagonists or antiheroes. Ernie would shake his head or cluck his tongue. "Chin up, kid," he'd say. "You can have whatever you want." She'd nod, and the three of them would bow their heads, as if beholding on the tabletop the very tableaux of these events, unified only by their inconclusiveness. Joe didn't exist for them, and there was nothing to discuss anyway; the relationship would never be anything more than it was.

Elaine picked a piece of orange pulp from her lower lip. "I'm thinking of going camping."

Ernie leaned forward. "Uh-oh, she's dating an outdoorsman."

Elaine let herself be teased. "He wants to go to Cumberland Island."

Her mother squinted at her. "Really," she said.

"Yup. That's what he said."

"Which one is this?" her mother asked.

"Joe," she said. "This one's Joe." But not her Joe. Her Joe didn't know from camping, and if he thought she did he never would have hooked up with her. Not the outdoorsy type, he'd said. Neither was she, really.

Ernie looked at her expectantly. "There's nothing new," she said. For a moment she considered telling Ernie and her mother about Joe, the real one. "I've got a guy who gives me pearls." But that sounded like the opening to a bad Jewish blues song.

"Camping, huh?" Ernie raised his arms again. "Amazing, isn't it, Alice?"

Alice's eyebrows lifted. "I'll say. My daughter was no Girl Scout."

Elaine excused herself to the bathroom. Inside she turned on the fan to block out Alice and Ernie's happy chatter. The butter-yellow ceramic tiles gleamed in the soft light. In the mirror, in her mother's bathroom in Chatham, her India-print dress reflected dully. Her collarbones protruded and her neck looked strained. Horizontal lines made their grim necklaces across her throat, and the skin there was papery, fragile. The short bob—so chunky and bright—looked perverse. The vintage dress and the dismal jute sandals—she squeezed her eyes shut and shoved her fists into the sockets. "Don't be stupid," she muttered. "Drink your drink. Be happy."

She returned to the table, her eyes throbbing. A muscle jumped in her right eyelid. Ernie regarded her closely. He pressed his lips together, and his face began to quiver. Alice placed her hand over his and spoke to Elaine. "It's the operation—and the drugs. He gets weepy."

Ernie wept openly, and Elaine gasped. "Ernie, what is it?"

"You never ask me favors anymore." He bawled into his lap. Alice knelt beside him and wrapped her arms around him.

"He's OK," she said. "You're OK—it's the drugs."

Elaine wracked her brain, trying to think of some favor. *Turn back the clock. Make me young again.* That would be in poor taste. She thought of Paul the dermatologist, of their dancing and subsequent dating. She had been fond of him.

Ernie managed to get control of himself. "But you have what you want." He wiped his eyes. "It's amazing, really, how you kids can imagine any kind of life for yourselves." He looked at Alice. "Not that I would want anything different."

"Of course not," Alice said. She put her head in his lap.

He turned to Elaine, his eyes filling again. "But you," he said, his voice husky, "you can have whatever you want."

Elaine touched the base of her throat and felt her cool fingers there. She realized she wouldn't cry. "I have," she said, "I have what I want."

A NOTE ON THE TYPE

The text of this book is set in ANDERSEN, named for the seventeenth-century founder Jan Andersen. Nils Pieter, an apprentice to Andersen, is credited with the design. The two shared a long correspondence after Pieter's apprenticeship, and the type appears to be based on Andersen's handwriting. The irregular shape of the serifs makes this type an impractical choice for most printed matter.

A NOTE ON THE TYPE

SUWANNEE MODERN was created in 1972 by Jonathan Howell. The Georgia native worked as a graphic artist in Manhattan, drawing advertisements for Bloomingdale's. He designed this type specifically for poster lettering. SUWANNEE MODERN enjoyed popularity during the 1980s among a group of women artists, whose guerrilla-style postering attracted the attention of Garment District workers and the homeless, who used the posters as bedsheets. A few of these posters have been collected to form a traveling exhibition, which has revived interest in this little-known movement. Most of the posters have been lost to time and the weather.

A NOTE ON THE TYPE

This book has been set in PRAGUE SANS SERIF, created in 1790 by the Dutch designer Bernard Kopland. The type is Kopland's attempt at Renaissance-style lettering; what is thought to be an earlier version was found, gouged and abraded, in the Utrecht attic studio where Kopland worked. Two workmen refitting the house for a young couple discovered the type. One workman pocketed the *W* and the *L*, for those were his girlfriend's initials. The other workman—the gasfitter—phoned the Historical Society, and this earlier version of PRAGUE SANS SERIF now resides, sans *W* and *L*, in the Historical Society's museum in Utrecht.

In his day, the clean lines of Kopland's design went largely unappreciated. The type is now prized for its quiet dignity, which imposes order on the chaos of postmodern text. Kopland never visited the city for which he named this type; records show he never left Utrecht. The circumstances surrounding his death by drowning at the age of thirty-eight remain unknown.

A NOTE ON THE TYPE

No one can pinpoint the exact provenance of UNIVERSAL HUMANES. The Roman type's easy readability made it popular for handbills early in the seventeenth century, and its use continued through the many mechanical revolutions in typesetting and design across centuries. Through many years of reproduction, small alterations to the type were introduced, most notably these: in 1780, the punch cutter Jan Ahlman, distracted by the imminent birth of his first grandchild, rushed the production of a set of type and inadvertently truncated the lowercase *a*'s serif; in 1829, William Quinn, whose eyes were going, enlarged the tittles of the *i* and *j*; later that century, Aloysius Jones, a recently freed slave, slanted the counter of the lowercase *e*; his daughter, Aretha Jones, made her own mark on the design in the early twentieth century by rotating the thinnest parts of the uppercase O from twelve and six to eleven and five. These alterations were faithfully reproduced by punch cutters and machinists, and were even copied or borrowed by other designers for their fonts, hoping to achieve the clarity and transparency of UNIVERSAL HUMANES. The current version of the type, which is still much admired, likely bears little resemblance to its model.

A NOTE ON THE TYPE

CYRILLIC BOOK comprises a suite of fonts intended to aid in the preservation of eastern European dialects. A group of scholars and designers worked together to prepare the font; their intent was to create a clean type that was easy to reproduce mechanically or digitally—on whatever equipment available. After a hopeful decade of implementation, most of the texts produced in this type were destroyed by fire. Some texts were found in mass graves, cleaned, and displayed in the Museum of Twentieth-Century Genocides until that building was destroyed under mysterious circumstances. The last living designer of CYRILLIC BOOK lives alone in San Diego and works mainly as a translator. He speaks to his relatives in Bosnia once a month. He no longer visits.

A NOTE ON THE TYPE

MONOLITH POST-VOX was created by Bert Fisher, a disciple of the artist and typeface designer Eric Gill. Fisher fell under Gill's thrall decades after Gill's death, while studying printmaking at the Rhode Island School of Design. Fisher became obsessed with Gill's assertion that typeface was a thing unto itself; it did not represent another thing, the way a painting or a photograph might. To honor his hero's maxim, Fisher endeavored to create an unreadable type, one that could not be used to transmit meaning in any language. In this he succeeded; most of the letters were unrecognizable, which violated Gill's basic principle—somehow overlooked by Fisher—that the skeletons of letters could not be fundamentally altered. At the opening exhibition of MONOLITH POST-VOX, one typeface designer exclaimed, "Fisher has broken the bones of the alphabet!" For a while, Fisher delighted in his bad-boy status, until an unknown art student made a discovery that undermined his manifesto. After minute examination, she found embedded in each letter a tableau, printed in relief. To the naked eye the design appeared abstract, but under magnification, each tableau could be discerned, and each contributed to a larger story, which could be read sequentially. Fisher had indeed hidden a representation within his typeface, a narrative that some believe autobiographical. Fisher has since dropped from view and is rumored to be teaching English in China.

A NOTE ON THE TYPE

CATSKILLS LINEALES debuted in the 1990s at the Catskills retreat of the artist and designer Alice Connaty and her husband, Marc Peary. The pair summered in a borrowed cabin with their two daughters for all fifteen years of their marriage. They worked via correspondence on the type, even while living together. This method caused delays in production, so that when the type was finally completed, the need for it had expired: the company that had hired the pair had gone out of business. Connaty and Peary's daughters projected the type onto old sheets and made sequential graphic narratives, which they hung in the trees throughout the woods. Neighbors and visitors delighted in these whimsical surprises. The sheets were left to deteriorate in the elements.

The daughters live a nomadic life, staying in rented or borrowed cabins all over the US, and they collaborate on installations in natural settings. Their ephemeral works often appear in the pages of popular art magazines. Individuals and corporations pay the women large sums of money to create work with a short life span for weddings, conferences, and the public offering of stocks. One of the daughters—each one blames the other—coined the phrase "epideictic installations," which helps some of their clients feel better about spending large sums of money on art that won't exist in a few months. Brides-to-be with a certain education and social standing recognize the sculptures as more sophisticated versions of organza bows and candles in hurricane lamps bedecked with ribbons in their colors. Couples pose for their engagement photos amid assemblages created by the two, and they send the photos to the *New York Times*. For these couples, the girls create entire landscapes for rehearsal dinners, weddings, and after-parties. They take no direction, only payment.

"You don't know if you're getting Long Island beachscape," said one bride-to-be, "or Mars."

Considerable competition has arisen to secure the duo's services. Brides compare photos and secretly rank the installations, finding reasons to favor their own. The daughters of Alice Connaty and Marc Peary are not troubled by any of this. They experience animal contentment when creating, so they work without ceasing.

Alice Connaty works as a life coach in Brooklyn. Marc Peary earns a living as a draftsman in Minneapolis. The two correspond regularly via the US Postal Service. Neither owns a cell phone, though they do converse on landlines. Alice Connaty owns a rotary phone from the 1940s, which she repaired herself, with help from a manual she checked out of the New York Public Library system. After twenty minutes of talking to her ex-husband, she laughs softly and tells him, "Marc, my wrist hurts! This phone is so heavy." Marc Peary still closes their conversations with the words "I love you," and Alice responds, "I love you, too."

A NOTE ON THE TYPE

No book has been set in this type. In fact, it isn't finished, and it has no name. JOSH, its creator, doesn't have as much time as he'd like to work on it. He usually puts in two or three hours after his eight-hour shift at Borders. His girlfriend, JENNA, also works at Borders. They both graduated from college last year, Jenna with a degree in music composition, Josh with a double major in poetics and drawing.

Josh isn't sure about this type. He likes it; he knows that. He's shown it to Jenna, and she likes it, too. It doesn't look like anything he's seen before, which excites him, when he lets himself think about it. He's relieved to have left his Art Nouveau phase behind, though it was important to go through that. He's trying not to worry about it. For now he's paying the bills, and the type is his secret. He has told his parents he is writing a book of criticism about contemporary epic poetry. "Contemporary epic poetry is hot," he tells his mother over the phone. "Unlimited potential for growth."

They rent a studio apartment to save money for their supplies. Josh works in an outbuilding—an old garage—that was supposed to have been torn down decades ago. The place smells of mold, motor oil, and dust, odors that appeal to him because he associates them with his work. When Jenna finishes with her composition for the evening, she fires up the hibachi, sets up two lawn chairs outside the garage door, and grills hot dogs or brownish beef or catfish—whatever is on sale at Winn-Dixie. She rations their beer. She hands him a sweating bottle. "Your mother's talking about a visit." He looks up from his work. "Let her." He knows she won't come. She doesn't understand that he hasn't given anything up.

At night, they nurse their beers and walk barefoot through the neighborhood. The frogs make a racket in the pond, and small rats wriggle and swirl on its banks. In the darkness, Josh sees letters floating, swooping in and out of his field of vision. He could shake his head to clear the images, but he doesn't. For a moment he wonders how much longer he and Jenna can go on. Will she tire of this life? Will he? How will it ever change? Jenna has been humming more or less the same tune. She retraces an auditory path, making little detours and variations. Her lips move, and her eyes are unfocused yet alert. He hears her work it out. She pulls her hand away from his and takes her music from her back pocket. She darts across the boulevard, wincing over small rocks and broken glass, to the illuminated steps of the community center. This is the best life they have known.

In the morning, they ride the bus to work with the community college students and mothers with babies on their way to day care, then jobs. They get coffee in the café before the store opens. Jenna puts on her nametag and heads off to Classics, where she hides from customers. Because her work is portable, she plays the How-Can-I-Make-This-Measure-Better game while she hides. She is the point person in Music for modern American composers, but no one ever asks about modern American composers. Josh loves that about her—that she has a passion for something hardly anyone cares about. He loves the way she walks around with her compositions folded lengthwise in the back pocket of her jeans. He loves the demented, possessed look that crosses her face when she is desperate to reach her hideout, before the sound escapes her. When he sees her this way, possessed by her work, he feels a roar inside him; he wants to circle around her, to guard the entrance to her cave in Classics. She looks like anyone, except for the dappled quality of alert dreaminess. No one knows who she is, but he has caught a glimpse of her. He can't wait to see what she will do.

———

Acknowledgments

I'm grateful and indebted to many, including the following:

To the editors of the journals in which these stories have appeared, my thanks for their encouragement: *Big Fiction:* "Three Portraits of Elaine Shapiro"; *The Cincinnati Review:* "Girls Come Calling," "Fine Arts," and "Word Problem"; *Consequence Magazine:* "History of Art" and "Repatriation"; *Fiction Southeast:* "Chinese Opera"; *Granta:* "The War Artist"; *The Lightship Anthology #3:* "The Confused Husband"; *Memorious:* "The War Artist Makes God Visible"; *The Rusty Toque:* "Exile"; *The Southern Review:* "A Note on the Type" (Autumn 2015); *Wraparound South:* "Magnolia Grandiflora."

To everyone at LSU Press, and especially to Michael Griffith and Susan Murray for their generous and careful attention to this manuscript.

To Miami University, the Ohio Arts Council, and the Provincetown Fine Arts Work Center.

To Terra Chalberg, for her guidance.

To writers who graciously read various parts and versions of this manuscript over the years: David Ebenbach, Chris Bachelder, Hugh Hunter, David O'Gorman, Martha Otis, Jody Bates, Joe Squance, Zack Hill, Bethany Pierce, Dana Leonard, Deanne Devine, John Morogiello, David Schloss, Larisa Breton, Erin Mc-Graw, and all the members of the FAWC summer workshops; and to the friends and family who helped with research: Jennifer Behrendt Dudas, Josh Russell, Ryan "Puddy" Hough, Gary Nicholson, Jim Rascati, Debora Greger; Brandy Kershner and Christina Carlton, for introducing me to Utrecht, my first glimpse of Europe. The errors and inadequacies are mine, not theirs.

To Billy, for his unflagging support.

Notes

Angela Gould's painting *1933 to 2002 in Blue Green* inspired the clock series described in "Magnolia Grandiflora."

These sources provided inspiration, information, and insight:

Carter, Sebastian. *Twentieth Century Type Designers.* New York: Norton, 1995.

Caxotte, Pierre, Jacques Perret, Rover Nimier, and Robert Descharnes. *Versailles que j'aime.* Paris: Éditions Sun, 1958.

Gough, Paul. *Stanley Spencer: Journey to Burghclere.* Bristol, UK: Sansom, 2006.

McCarthy, Fiona. *Stanley Spencer: An English Vision.* New Haven, CT: Yale University Press, 1997.

Zim, Herbert S., and Ira N. Gabrielson. *A Guide to the Most Familiar American Birds.* Golden Nature Guide. New York: Golden Press, 1949.